OPERATOR 5:
THE RED INVADER

THE RED INVADER

By Curtis Steele

STEEGER BOOKS • 2020

CHAPTER 1
CRATER OF DOOM

THE RED and green and white lights of a lone airplane twinkled in the snow-driven sky, far above the whitened wilderness of the Pennsylvania hills. Slowly it traced sparkling circles in the heavens while the drone of its motor throbbed far into the vast darkness. It hovered above a desolate region where constant danger lurked.

Danger—because these rugged hills lay today untouched by civilization, though reached to the limits of cosmic space.

In spite of the triple peril, the solitary airplane shuttled its way across the zenith. Snow beat back from its propeller, packing upon the helmeted heads of the three persons in the pits. The cold-cramped pilot glanced back at his two passengers repeatedly, hoping to see the signal that would send him driving back toward Roosevelt Field—but that signal did not come. Steadily, interminably, the plane traced its circles on the heavens.

In the second cubby a young man, garbed in fur-lined coveralls, leaned across the cowling with binoculars pressed to his eyes, goggles raised. He peered intently down into the depths of the darkness. His attitude was alert, his manner determined. He scarcely moved as snow flurried around him—as the plane banked and weaved.

This young man, in the secret archives of the United States Intelligence Service, was designated Operator 5.

James Christopher—his name was as much of a secret as the nature of his undercover activities—turned to the shortwave radio installation in the passenger-pit, plugged the tips of a flexible cord into two pin-jacks. He brought a microphone close to his lips and spoke quietly: "Calling M-11. Calling M-11."

The words were invisible lightning flashing through the

night; immediately an answer rang in the ear-'phones in his helmet: "M-11. Z-7 talking."

The deep, resonate voice was that of the chief of all United States Intelligence activities. Not even to Operator 5, his most valued undercover agent, was he known by any name other than Z-7. Through the ether, Jimmy Christopher asked him quietly: "Chief, has Operator J-4 reported?"

One instant, at the stroke of twelve, transformed Times Square into a scene of carnage and chaos!

"Not since six o'clock, my boy. We have had no word since his message that he had located Radi Havara."

"He was to have reported again at seven, without fail, Chief. It is past seven now."

"Yes. His silence worries me—for excellent reasons, as you well know."

"When that report comes, Chief," Jimmy Christopher went on quietly, "please flash me at once."

"I will. In the meantime—I'm completely mystified about this flight you are making into Pennsylvania, Operator 5. Why are you taking this dangerous chance? Can it possibly have some connection with the woman spy?"

"SINCE WE received word that Radi Havara has smuggled herself into the country, Chief," Operator 5 answered, "I have felt that any unusual occurrence will bear investigating. We can't overlook a single chance at learning the purpose behind her coming to the United States. Perhaps I'm off on a wild goose chase, Z-7, but I think not. More than that I can't say until I have something definite to report."

"Very well." Z-7's voice echoed in the ear-'phones. "But watch yourself! I don't need to warn you that Radi Havara is the most dangerous espionage agent active today. If you hit upon a lead, by all means flash me at once."

Operator 5 cleaned the snow from the lenses of his binoculars, turned them downward again. Beneath lay bleak, endless hills, thick with snow-laden trees—an almost impenetrable wilderness. He leaned motionless over the cowling, intent, alert.

His lips began to tighten with a growing hopelessness, but he persisted with the strange search.

An apparently pointless report, carried by teletype into Headquarters M-11 of the United States Intelligence Service in New York, had sent Jimmy Christopher into this dangerous air. It was a brief bit of information that had won no more than a glance from Z-7, but Operator 5 had studied it curiously. It was tucked in his pocket now, a few brief lines that might have gone into a file of miscellany and become lost:

> ... M-11... GIANT METEOR REPORTED WEST OF WILLIAMS-PORT, PENN., JUST AFTER DARK... FLASH SEEN AND POWERFUL CONCUSSIONS FELT OVER WIDE AREA BUT EXACT POINT OF STRIKE NOT DETERMINED... METEOR MUST BE ONE OF LARGEST EVER TO HIT THE EARTH....

Operator 5 had not explained to Z-7 his reason for immediately chartering a plane from Roosevelt Field. He had not disclosed the purpose of his strange search. For more than an hour he had been droning through the bitter wind, scanning the rugged ground, urged by a grim curiosity. A second hour was almost past before a hint of success came to him. Lights flashed through the lenses of his binoculars. They were dim sparkles through the veil of snow, shining points that swung and jerked. His nerves tightened; he turned to consult a map thumb-tacked in the cubby; he peered overside again to study the spots gleaming in an unsettled territory.

"Lower!" he commanded his pilot. "Motor off! Keep above those lights!"

The plane soughed down, the gun of the radial cut. The snow-flecked wings rocked in the rough air as the crate glided. Jimmy Christopher followed the lights below with his glasses, tightened as he glimpsed dark movements in the shine—movements as though men were shifting about hurriedly. He straightened to say quietly through the whirring of the wind: "I think we will find something very interesting down there, Tim."

OPERATOR 5'S companion in the pit was a boy in his teens whose eyes sparkled eagerly through the frosted lenses of his goggles. Because he was too young to pass the requirements, Tim Donovan was not a member of the Intelligence Service, but in the past he had rendered valuable aid to Jimmy Christopher. Side by side they had worked to penetrate the sinister mysteries of vitally important cases. Repeatedly the boy had demonstrated his unbounded courage as an unofficial assistant to Operator 5. No accredited under-cover agent could be depended upon more fully than Tim Donovan.

"Gee; Jimmy, I can't figure out why you're so interested in a falling star," he declared puzzledly. "Do you think those lights means that somebody's found where it hit?"

"I think those lights mean a good deal more, Tim," Operator 5 answered quietly. "A good deal more. They may mean that—"

He broke off, peering again through his binoculars, adjusting the focus. In the field of vision he perceived a ragged, round area of black in an expanse of ground that was elsewhere blanketed with fresh snow. He studied it carefully, noting that the spots of light were moving around it at distant points. He straightened again to slap his pilot's shoulder.

"A road passes close to the lights. Keep your beacons off and try to make a landing on it!"

The pilot stared down and blurted: "Good Lord, that's a long chance! The road may not be wide enough to put the plane down in and it's probably rough as the devil. If we crack up we'll starve before we can get out of this country!"

"Try to make the landing," Operator 5 insisted, "and make it as quietly as possible!"

Tim Donovan clung to the rail, watching Operator 5, as the plane's glide grew swifter. Wind, laden with snow, slashed past the wings as bleak territory blurred below. Jimmy Christopher continued to gaze through his glasses, until the plane swooped so low that the snow-banked trees cut off the gleams of the ground lights.

"Half a dozen men," Operator 5 declared quietly to the anxious boy, "are doing something with instruments. They seem to be very interested in the spot where the meteor fell—if it was a meteor—and so am I. Steady, Tim! Hang on!"

The plane was rocking down to the narrow, cleared strip of road which wound through the rugged slope. It was a lane of gleaming white amid thick-growing trees, a twining threat of destruction. In the fore-pit, the pilot tensed at his controls, head lowered into the driving snow.

The wing-tips slashed down between the trees flanking the road. Snow spilled silently from laden branches as the crate floated past. Wavering, rocking, the trucks cut downward, gash-ing through the soft whiteness. Suddenly the fuselage jarred; the tail slapped down. Brakes pressed hard upon spinning drums, and the plane slid to a stop.

The pilot straightened back with a breath. "God! I never thought we'd make it! Getting down in—"

"Quiet!" Operator 5 whispered with a nudge at the pilot's shoulder. "Stay here—wait. Tim—come with me."

Jimmy Christopher eased over the cowling, dropped into the fluffy white. Tim Donovan scrambled down beside him as he bent to examine the snow. The trucks of the plane had made wavering streaks on the road, but beyond, Jimmy Christopher found deep-pressed tracks. He studied them, straightened, peered across the slope.

"A truck came up this road a little while ago, Tim," he said quietly. "There's very little fresh snow in the tracks. It must be somewhere above now."

Tim Donovan asked quietly: "What're you going to do, Jimmy?"

"Take a look, first of all," Operator 5 answered, "at the spot where that so-called meteor fell."

HE SIGNALED the boy to follow as he trudged through banked snow, off the road. Ducking under laden branches, zigzagging, he worked his way across rugged ground with Tim at his heels. He paused abruptly, peering at indentations in the white—a line of footprints crossing his path at an angle. Two men had made the tracks; they led deeper down the slope. And in that direction, faintly, lights were flickering through bent branches.

Quietly, Jimmy Christopher went on. When he paused again it was at a point where the snow was tramped down by a maze of prints. In the midst of the trodden area was a heap of untrampled white. Inspecting it, Operator 5 found three holes in that area, each round and as large as a half-dollar, placed in a triangle. He said quietly:

"Some sort of a tripod was set up here."

He proceeded more cautiously, toward a bank of blackness that loomed against the freshness of the snow beyond. As he approached it, he found stones that had rolled, others that had dropped into the white bed, and a dusting of black earth. Pausing again, he gazed across a pit of black, raw dirt—a conical crater whose walls were studded with loosened rock.

Tim Donovan exclaimed: "That's where the meteor hit, Jimmy!"

"It was not a meteor, Tim," Jimmy Christopher answered in a whisper. "Not a meteor.... Notice that smell. It is burned high explosive, Tim."

"Explosive?" the boy questioned. "Gee, Jimmy! If a falling star didn't make this hole, what did?"

Operator 5's hand shot out to the boy's arm. "Quiet, Tim! Back!" He whirled, tugging the boy after him. They ducked behind a clump of evergreens laden with snow. Crouching, Operator 5 peered through the whitened branches at lights flickering brightly not far away. The gleam of a lantern shafted across the white and voices sounded as the snow crunched under moving feet. From behind the circular mound of black, two men appeared.

One was carrying the light; the other was shouldering an instrument affixed to a folded tripod. They paused within ten yards of the trees behind which Operator 5 and Tim Donovan were crouching. One spread the legs of the tripod, steadied it; he swung the tubular instrument affixed to its apex toward another light gleaming farther away. As Jimmy Christopher watched, the distant lantern swung as if in signal.

Operator 5 touched Tim Donovan's arm in warning, rose. His hand slipped into the pocket of his coveralls, and he lifted an automatic. Quietly, he stepped away from the trees, the boy following noiselessly. They saw the lights swing again. The man with the tripod instrument hunched to peer through the tube. The two men were so intent upon their work that Operator 5 approached within two yards of them without making them aware of his presence.

His automatic was covered and hidden as he watched them. When he spoke, his voice was a startling sound in the silence. "Why are you men surveying this crater?"

The man at the instrument straightened with a gasp, but his head did not turn. The other stood rigid, his lantern swinging slightly. They were wearing heavy overcoats; their collars were turned up to shield their faces. Operator 5's automatic turned slowly toward them as he spoke again.

"Your reason, gentlemen, for surveying this crater—what is it?"

Jimmy Christopher's answer was the thunder and lightning of blasting guns.

THE TWO men whirled at the same instant. The lantern

spun from the hand of one, became a streak of dazzling light that flashed toward Operator 5's head. Tim Donovan cried a startled warning an instant before the first shot sounded. The gun blazed into the darkness that swept down when the lantern plunged into a snowbank and sizzled out. A rocking fusillade crashed out of the night.

Jimmy Christopher leaped aside, snatching at Tim Donovan's arm, whirling the boy so violently that he spun off balance into the snow. He leaped across the boy, his own automatic splashing flame. A cry of rage rang across the slope. Flitting shadows moved against the background of the whitened trees—the two men separating. Jimmy Christopher released lead again, aiming swiftly at the flashing light of an exploding gun.

"Stay down, Tim!" he ordered, and sprang again.

Ringing shouts carried across the slope from beyond the black crater. Operator 5 dropped to one knee, sent a singing bullet after one fluttering shadow that vanished behind the banked trees. From a point yards away, the second gun cracked out a bullet that tugged at the shoulder of Operator 5's coveralls. His automatic spat again, and a choking cry sounded. The man who had fired fell face down in fluffy white and lay motionless.

Jimmy Christopher sprang up. He commanded: "Stick close, Tim!" and broke into a run across the slope. No lights were flashing now near the black mound that ringed the deep crater; every lantern had been extinguished. Rapidly, confusedly, footfalls crunched through the snow as men ran. Operator 5 sprinted, gun ready for instant use, swinging toward the road. He paused abruptly as a loud, metallic snarl sounded.

11

It was the starter of a car going into action; a motor snorted. The sounds came from down the slope. Operator 5 bounded forward again. When he reached the open lane of the road, he glimpsed a moving blackness beyond that vanished—a sedan, whisking from sight around a bend, lights out. The vibrant sound of its powerful motor rapidly moved away; and Operator 5 sprinted along the road, paused.

"No good trying to chase it!" he exclaimed to Tim Donovan as the boy burst into the open. "Tim—are you all right?"

"Never touched me, Jimmy!" Tim blurted. "Gee—what were they doing? What does it mean, Jimmy?"

"It means," Operator 5 answered cryptically, "that the so-called meteor has become very important to us, Tim!"

He paused, his blue eyes narrowing with thought, and again bent to examine the huge tire-tracks in the road. He was certain they had not been made by the sedan which had carried the unknown men from the spot; they indicated that a truck had climbed higher into the hills and had not returned. Straightening, Operator 5 walked with Tim Donovan up the slope, toward the spot where the plane had landed.

"There may be enough men in that truck to out-number us hopelessly, Tim," he said, as he explained the situation. "They have probably heard the shots—"

His voice trailed off as he broke into a run. The waiting plane loomed black around a bend in the road. The pilot had climbed out; he trotted toward Operator 5 breathlessly.

"Good Lord, what happened? I heard the shots. I thought maybe you'd been—"

Jimmy Christopher cut him off with a gesture. "You're going back up," he declared, "without us—right now!"

"Without you?" The pilot gulped. "How the devil will you get out of this wilderness if I leave you behind? You're taking a chance of freezing and starving if—"

"You're going up right now," Operator 5 reiterated, "without us. Head east—get out of this country. At the end of an hour, turn back. When you come back, keep your lights out and watch the roads. I'll signal you with a flashlight. Got it straight?"

THE BAFFLED pilot shrugged, climbed into the pit of the plane. Operator 5 and Tim Donovan stood back as the cranked motor burst into a roar. Snow flew in the slipstream as the pilot settled anxiously to the controls. His head wagged; the task of taking-off from the snowy, curved lane was a grave danger. He sent the plane crawling until the angle of the slope decreased. Then he opened the gun and the motor howled back flying white as the plane plunged.

Operator 5 watched it intently. Its tail lifted; it swung dangerously; suddenly it swooped. With consummate skill, the pilot flung it into the clear air above the tree-tops flanking the road. Immediately it zoomed, then banked; its lights twinkled through the swirling flakes as it turned its nose eastward. In the darkness, Operator 5 and Tim Donovan watched it as it became lost in the storm, as the drone of its motor began to fade into the silence.

"Jimmy—gee!" Tim Donovan exclaimed as he peered about. "Why'd you send that plane away?"

"For the benefit of the men in that truck, wherever it is, Tim," Operator 5 explained. "They'll think we've left, possibly to chase the other car. We're playing a waiting game, old-timer—and we've got to keep out of sight."

Jimmy Christopher turned off the road, and the boy followed. They plunged through heavy drifts and followed the line of footprints that led toward the heaped ring of black fringing the deep, dark crater. Operator 5 paused at the spot where the gun-fight had occurred. Grimly he turned the fallen man face-up from the snow that was reddened. Quietly he said:

"No explanation will ever come from him, Tim. He was a bad target in this darkness. A surveyor. There is his transit."

"You mean these men were measuring the crater, Jimmy?" Tim asked puzzledly.

"Perhaps not that, old-timer. Rather, I think they were determining its exact location. Why—is very important for us to know."

"Then it wasn't a meteor at all, Jimmy!"

"Not a meteor at all," Operator 5 answered in a low tone. "It was a shell. A high explosive projectile that—"

He broke off, listening, peered toward the road. Tim swung also to listen. Through the quiet of the hills came a churning sound, a quiet clanking. The noise of the airplane exhaust had vanished; now there was no other disturbance of the quiet. Jimmy Christopher's lips tightened in a smile.

"Our subterfuge is working, Tim! The truck is coming back down!"

He ducked past the whitened trees, and the boy followed quickly. The noises continued until they reached the evergreens banking the road. There they dropped into a crouch and waited.

The noises grew louder each second; abruptly, from around a bend in the lane above, appeared the crawling black mass of a huge truck. Its lights were out; its wheels were chained. It rolled slowly, tracking the snow deeply. It was completely enclosed. Operator 5 and Tim Donovan remained motionless, watching it, as it approached and clattered past. Jimmy Christopher's hand went to the boy's arm. "After it, Tim! Jump the running-board on this side, but keep out of sight. Quick!"

THEY DUCKED through the trees, onto the road, when the truck was a few yards past. Operator 5 ran to its far side. He noted, as he passed the rear end, that a heavily-insulated black wire was trailing through the snow behind it. A glance upward showed him that another wire was supported above its top. He glimpsed Tim Donovan racing along the near side. He reached out, gripped a rod, and swung himself up.

He hung down outside the door of the driver's compartment. Gradually he raised himself, peered through the frosted pane. The man at the wheel was mufflered, bending forward intently to study the dark road. Operator 5 quickly slipped his automatic into his free hand.

He twisted the handle quickly, straightened, gripping the wheel and thrusting out his automatic. A burst of air came from the startled driver's lips. He jerked his right arm as though to draw a gun. Operator 5 warned: "Steady!" and pulled himself in.

He dropped his automatic; he thrust stiffened fingers against the side of the driver's neck. Another breathy gasp sounded as the man stiffened. Operator 5 toppled him aside, steadied the wheel. He slipped to the seat, sent the truck crawling around a bend, and turned to inspect the driver. The man was unconscious, rigid; the swift jiu-jitsu blow of Operator 5 had paralyzed him. Satisfied that he would remain dead to the world for at least an hour, Jimmy Christopher reached to open the farther door of the driver's cubby.

"In, Tim!" he whispered. "Take the wheel!"

The startled boy pulled onto the seat; his eyes shone round as he took control of the truck. His one hand gripped the brake-lever to keep the truck from gathering momentum down the slope as he steadied the wheel with the other. Operator 5 eased across him, recovering the automatic and peering at the front wall of the truck body.

He saw the cracks of a door that opened above the driver's seat. He gripped the handle, raised the latch noiselessly. With the utmost care, he opened the small door a crack; a gleam of light shone outward. Jimmy Christopher peered through it, motionless, as Tim Donovan gripped the wheel and glanced at him anxiously.

In the shine of light in the interior of the truck he saw other surveying instruments leaning in a corner. From another door, at the rear of the body, snowy foot-tracks showed, as though one of the men surprised at the crater had hurried into it. Opening the door wider, bit by bit, Jimmy Christopher glimpsed a table bolted against the side wall. Over that table the light was shining; in front of a short-wave radio installation, a man in a bulky great-coat was hunched.

The man at the radio was scribbling on a pad of paper. His hand raised to make adjustments of the knobs on the black panels. He checked the settings quickly; he tapped on a sending-key. With uncanny soundlessness, Operator 5 thrust the door wide and slipped through. Two quick steps took him to the table; his hand shot out to snap a switch.

Instantly, the man at the table whirled up. Through thick eyeglasses his eyes widened with desperate fear. He drove out a huge fist as Operator 5 side-stepped. Jimmy Christopher's gun flashed steady and his voice rang.

"Back up! Away from the table!"

A WILD frenzy shone in the eyes of the big man as he frantically grabbed at the gun in Operator 5's hand. Jimmy Christopher thrust him back. The tremendous weight of the big man was a crushing force against Operator 5. As the truck jolted, as the huge body swayed, they struggled with silent savagery. Operator 5 refrained from using his automatic; he drove out swift, straight blows with his free hand—jabs that forced the huge man back, sent him stumbling to the rear end of the truck.

In desperate defiance of Operator 5's automatic, the man jerked a revolver from the pocket of his great coat. Jimmy Christopher leaped the length of the truck, snatched at the wrist of the hand holding the gun. The big man wrenched away desperately, and a jolt of the truck body flung Operator 5 against him. They sprawled together into the corner—and the muffled crash of a shot sounded.

Grimly Operator 5 drew himself up. Swaying, he stood peering down at the huddled figure in the corner. The big man's head was lolling, his hand unclenched to drop the gun. Smoke wisped from its bore, and a charred patch showed on the big coat almost

17

above the breast. Coldly Jimmy Christopher tore the coat open to discover a ragged wound—to discover that the accidental discharge had stilled the huge man's heart.

His eyes grew dark as he peered about. He stepped to the table and took up the sheets of paper scrawled by the man now dead. He heard an anxious cry—"Jimmy! Jimmy!" and jerked open the front door of the van.

"Okay, Tim!" he said breathlessly. "Keep the truck going! When you hit the main road—"

"Looks like it's just ahead, Jimmy!" the boy blurted, peering back. "Gosh, for a minute I thought—"

"Steady, old-timer! When the plane comes back, use this light and flash a signal. We want that crate again!"

Operator 5 turned back to the radio table. Grimly he compared the scrawled sheets, and saw that the big man had hastily translated a message into a code. He read the loosely-written words as a dread came to fill him—a dread of a sinister unknown:

R.H. Point of burst the message began, and the words were followed by symbols indicating a position by latitude and longitude to the fraction of a second. *Accuracy perfect. We need wait no longer.*

Operator 5's fingertips tapped the table as he studied the message. Inspecting the radio equipment, he found that it was convertible to voice transmission. Quickly he snapped switches that threw a microphone into the circuit, trimmed the oscillator to the wavelength of Headquarters M-11 in New York.

"Calling M-11! No distorter! Calling M-11!"

Operator 5 affixed ear-'phones and heard Z-7's voice come out of the ether.

"I've been waiting anxiously to hear from you! I have a report concerning J-4! He was found dead—stabbed in the heart—in Herald Square not ten minutes ago! Stabbed in the heart like the others we detailed to trail Radi Havara! Good God—ordering our men to shadow that woman has become equivalent to murdering them! Four of our best agents murdered and each—"

"Chief!" Operator 5 interrupted ringingly. "I have a report that can wait—and orders! I am returning to New York as soon as possible. I want to see J-4's body. No one is to search it until I arrive. That's important, Chief—more important than you realize!"

While the truck jolted over the mountain road, Operator 5 peered at the huge man who lay on the floor.

He read again the message that a hand now dead had flashed to some unknown point through the ether, and his eyes grew dark. Soundlessly his lips formed the sinister words:

"We need wait no longer!"

CHAPTER 2
DAUGHTER OF SATAN

THE GOLD-LEAF name on the windows was *Marielle*. Behind the polished panes, exquisite gowns were displayed against a background of velvet draperies. Through the bronze door passed a parade of women of wealth to lounge in deep chairs, to smoke imported scented cigarettes, to choose costly creations worn by manikins of exquisite figure and perfect grace. At lofty prices, Marielle offered her clients the acme of styled beauty in gowns.

Yet, behind that gorgeous establishment, unknown to the clients who came to the salon, lay rooms and offices devoted to a purpose far different from clothing the feminine figure. The men who entered and left the hidden suite quietly were interested not at all in satins and silks. They were undercover agents; Marielle's establishment masked the location of secret Intelligence Headquarters M-11.

A month ago these rooms had been deserted; a month hence they might again be empty, but now they hummed with busy activity. The communications-room handled a steady flow of messages by teletype, telephone, cable and radio. Trusted assistants worked incessantly to keep up-to-the-minute every item on file in scores of fireproof cabinets—items duplicated in every other secret Intelligence headquarters in the nation. M-11 was a subsidiary of the central Headquarters WDC-13 in Washington, D.C., but Z-7's presence in New York now gave it an importance greater than any other.

Code words took Operator 5 and Tim Donovan past the sentries at the doors. They had flown to New York in the plane that had returned to the Pennsylvania hills for them; from Roosevelt Field Jimmy Christopher had driven in his Diesel-engined roadster. Together they strode into the inner room, walled with filing-cabinets, which was Z-7's office.

The gray-clad, grim-faced man rose to grip Operator 5's hand.

His dark eyes glittered with deep lights as he studied Jimmy Christopher's face.

"You have hit upon something important, I know!" he declared. "If it has any connection with Radi Havara—"

"It has, Chief," Operator 5 declared. "She has been in the United States only a short time, and already some plan of espionage is in operation. We have all other undercover agents under observation—she alone can be responsible for what is happening. So far we have only a hint of the nature of her operations—but for some reason, a high-explosive projectile was fired into the Pennsylvania hills tonight and—"

"A shell?" Z-7 interrupted. "Are you sure of that? Where did it come from?"

Jimmy Christopher answered. "We cannot even guess now. A report of its point of burst was being sent by wireless immediately afterward in order to check up on the accuracy of the gun—sent to Radi Havara. It was, I'm sure, a test shot!"

"I don't understand!" Z-7 exclaimed. "Why should some hidden big gun be tested in such a way? What does it mean? What will follow?"

Operator 5 placed on the chief's desk the scrawled pages he had brought from the radio-equipped truck.

"The answers to those questions, Chief, are known only to Radi Havara," he declared. "Perhaps, leaving the answers to them is the reason why four of our best agents have been murdered while trailing that woman. Chief—was J-4 brought here?"

"Yes. I have followed your orders. If you wish to see him now—"

21

Z-7 LED the way into a corridor, opened a door. Operator 5 stepped through and Tim Donovan followed while Z-7 withdrew. They stopped short, staring at a cot on which the still form of a man lay. The boy's eyes widened; Operator 5's lips pressed hard. There was a metallic glitter in the light—a reflection from the knife-blade driven deep into the heart of the cadaver on the cot.

"J-4," Operator 5 said quietly. "One of our best men. The fourth ordered to trail Radi Havara—the fourth to die with a knife in his heart."

The boy blurted: "Gee, Jimmy! Who is Radi Havara? Why was she trailed?"

"Radi Havara?" Jimmy Christopher's tone was low. "She is the cleverest espionage agent operating today, Tim. She is as merciless as a panther, as deadly as a cobra. She is involved in such a web of international intrigue that it is impossible to know which nation she is serving. We know only three things about her.

"First, she smuggled herself into the United States a few weeks ago and at this moment is keeping herself under cover somewhere in New York. Second, she is linked directly with the deaths of our Operators H-8, M-4 and C-92—and now J-4. Third, her presence is a threat to the security of the United States—a menace impossible to exaggerate."

Operator 5 stepped quietly to J-4's still body. His fingers moved with deft swiftness from pocket to pocket. When he straightened, he was holding a small leather-covered notebook. A detached slip between two of the pages attracted his attention.

He was studying the lines written upon it when Tim Donovan observed:

"Jimmy, I've read in the papers about three dead men being found in the streets—but I didn't know they were Intelligence operators."

"Not only were they Intelligence men, Tim, but each one was trying to locate Radi Havara, and they all died in the same strange way. When we first received word from F-31, one of our agents in London, that the woman spy had left England with the intention of smuggling herself into the United States, H-8 was assigned the job of locating her. He found her here in New York with surprising ease."

Operator 5 turned his lenses slowly through the snow-flecked haze of light. "Apparently Radi Havara was making no attempt to hide herself completely. She would appear openly at a night-club, a theatre, or at one of a score of swanky bars. She would slip away, only to turn up at another. H-8 did not arrest her at once because his orders were to locate her headquarters if possible. No doubt he succeeded—but at the cost of his life."

"He was the first of the three found dead in the streets, Jimmy?" Tim Donovan asked excitedly.

"The first, Tim. Stabbed through the heart. His body crushed, as though he had fallen from a great height. The report of his death declared that he had been thrown from a high window of a skyscraper at Forty-second and Fifth Avenue—after the knife had been driven into his heart. Yet the investigation proved that he had not entered that building."

"Then the same thing happened to the second operator who was put on the job!" Tim Donovan exclaimed.

"EXACTLY THE same thing. He located Radi Havara in the Barbary Coast Club, and trailed her. After his first report by telephone, he was never heard from again. Hours later—early in the morning—his crushed body was found, a knife thrust through the heart, in the court of the RCA Building, in Radio City. And again the investigation proved that M-4 had not entered that building."

Tim blurted: "He might've been dropped from an airplane, Jimmy!"

Operator 5's blue eyes took on a darker tone.

"No, Tim. There isn't any point within Manhattan from which an airplane can take-off, and it's too much to suppose that the dead bodies were carried away, to some secret airfield, only for the purpose of dropping them into town. It's certain, too, that an autogyro was not used. There are very few roofs from which an autogyro can take off. If one attempted it, it would certainly be heard and spotted. Another thing—any airplane would have to fly higher above Manhattan than the condition of the bodies indicated. That is, they fell from a lower level than an airplane could have gone without being seen. And the circumstances surrounding C-2's death make it even stranger."

"He was the one found in Central Park, Jimmy?"

"Yes. He dropped directly in front of a line of cars near the exit of the park at 110th street and Seventh Avenue. It was early in the morning and there were only a few lights. C-2 came out of the empty air—out of the sky—and dropped directly in front of several cars."

"Gee, Jimmy!" the boy exclaimed. "You think—?"

"I think," Operator 5 interrupted briskly, "that it is high time we ceased sacrificing valuable men to the ruthlessness of Radi Havara."

He turned to the door. It opened as he approached it. Z-7 stepped grimly into the room. He raised a finger to point toward a table that sat in darkness against the wall.

"There, Operator 5," he said, "at last is the explanation of how the bodies of our agents were disposed of. Look at it—as devilish a contrivance for covering a murder as has ever been used."

Jimmy Christopher stepped close to the table and bent above a billowing pile of oiled silk. He noted a peculiar clockwork mechanism at one side, with a rope attached. His inspection went on as Z-7 explained:

"A balloon. It was inflated and released—from what spot God only knows! J-4—as well as the other three men—were carried up into the air by it, already dead. A hook was fastened in the coat-collar of the dead body. The time-clock arrangement released the hook, allowed the body to fall. In the three previous cases, the balloons, of course, sprang higher into the air and were lost. In the case of J-4, the clock failed to release the hook, and the balloon came down with him. These men were killed because they discovered Radi Havara's headquarters—and she chose that diabolical method of disposing of the bodies so as to keep her whereabouts hidden."

Operator 5 nodded. "Chief, I think I have a clue to Radi

Havara's headquarters. It may be a trick—a false lead—but I must follow it. The sooner I see it through, the better."

Z-7 looked startled as Operator 5 strode from the room. He followed, with Tim Donovan, into the office beyond. There Jimmy Christopher took up a telephone. The number he called was that of the home of his father, ex-Operator Q-6. The voice that answered was a girl's.

"Di!" Operator 5 said quickly, "I need your help."

"Jimmy Christopher," came the prompt answer, "you know I'll do anything in the world to help you!"

DIANE ELLIOT'S statement carried conviction. She, like Operator 5, was in her early twenties; but her alert intelligence, her courage, her unbeatable persistence had already won her an enviable position as special correspondent for the far-flung Amalgamated Press, one of the greatest news-services in the world. She had, in past cases, aided Jimmy Christopher to the limit of her considerable ability. Her supreme interest was in gathering news; his supreme necessity was secrecy; but they worked together in perfect harmony.

"You'll have to move fast, Di," Operator 5 told the girl crisply. "Hop into a taxi, get to the Montblanc Hotel as fast as you can make it, and wait for me at the entrance."

"I'm on my way right now!"

Operator 5 turned from the telephone to gaze at Z-7. "Chief," he said, "I have reason to believe Radi Havara is staying at the Montblanc—and I'm going there."

"I can't allow you to go there alone!" Z-7 protested. "With

four men already murdered by that ruthless woman, I can't take the chance of allowing you—"

"Tim will be with me, chief, and Di," Operator 5 interrupted. "They're the equal of any two operators you might assign to go with me. I'll have to tackle this in my own way. I may not be following a clue so much as walking into a trap—but it must be done."

"My boy! What do you mean?"

"Radi Havara is cooking a veritable devil's brew, chief. While that daughter of Satan is at work, we must play a dangerous game and at least be sure of our chances when we play them. Perhaps you'll find me dropping out of the sky with a knife in my heart, chief—but I'm going."

Z-7's face grew pale. Tim Donovan's eyes sought Jimmy Christopher's anxiously as they strode to the door. They passed through hidden entrances, emerged upon the quiet street. Operator 5 slipped behind the wheel of the roadster which was waiting at the curb and the boy clambered in beside him.

Operator 5 opened the little black notebook he had taken from J-4's body. He read a hurriedly-penciled address: *R.H. Hotel Montblanc, 1521-2.* He raised from between the leaves the bit of folded paper; he inhaled its heavy, exotic fragrance.

"Evidently," he said, "carried in a woman's purse," and he read its terse, enigmatic message:

TIME FIRST MIDNIGHT TONIGHT EVERY TWELVE THEREAFTER. V-44.

He glanced at his wrist watch. It was exactly 11:45 p.m.

27

The motor of the roadster sang its song of power as Jimmy Christopher shot it from the drifted curb.

NEAR THE snow-laden marquee of the Hotel Montblanc, on Park Avenue, Operator 5 swung his roadster to a stop. Tim Donovan walked briskly with him toward the entrance. In the flecked shine of the lights Diane Elliot was waiting, her fur collar turned high against richly red cheeks and redder lips. She smiled and stepped to Operator 5's side. "On the job, Jimmy!"

"As always, Di. Your part in this little visit won't take long, but it's important. Stay with me."

"Right with you," Diane complied.

They strode into a gold and green lobby, to the bronze doors of the elevators. There silently, they waited while an indicator marked the descent of a cage. When the grille slid open, Jimmy Christopher, about to step forward, stopped short. Under his breath he ordered tersely: "Wait!"

One passenger stepped from the cab—a woman. She was a dazzling beauty. Her perfect coiffure was black and bright as a raven's wing; her skin was white and smooth as alabaster; her dark eyes were brilliant, her color high. She held an ermine wrap close about her supple figure as she turned toward the entrance.

Operator 5 quietly followed. The frank admiration in his eyes was clouded by a deepening darkness as he stepped from the entrance behind the woman. At the curb the uniformed starter shrilled a whistle; a cab spurted into the glare. Operator 5 paused to whisper: "Tim! Around to the far side of that cab! Get the address she gives the driver if you can. Di, wait here until I signal!"

Her one delicate hand lifting the trailing flair of her cloth-of-gold gown, exposing slender ankles and jeweled slippers, the woman stepped toward the car. Tim Donovan, obeying Jimmy Christopher's quick orders, hurried past the rear of the taxi as she entered it. She leaned forward and spoke to the driver; she settled back as the motor hummed. At that instant Jimmy Christopher strode forward. He twisted open the door. He bowed, and said quietly: "Good evening, Miss Havara."

The woman's dark eyes turned full into his face. For a moment they remained impassive; for a moment her expression did not change. Slowly, then, her lips curved into a smile. Her voice was low and soft: "Good evening, Mr. Christopher."

Operator 5's eyes sharpened. He in turn smiled. "You know me, then."

"We know," the woman said slowly, "each other."

Operator 5 bowed again. "Evidently! Since we seem to be old friends, though we've never seen each other, I hope you will pardon my intrusion."

"Of course. I've been expecting you."

Jimmy Christopher's smile did not waver. He asked, with the utmost politeness: "Expecting me?"

"I hope I do not flatter myself," Radi Havara answered, "by believing that my presence here should be of deep interest to a man of your caliber, Mr. Christopher."

"You flatter yourself," Operator 5 declared promptly, "not at all. I should say, on the contrary, that your presence merits the interest of a far abler man than I, Miss Havara."

The woman laughed softly. "Your modesty is quite charming.

I am quite sure that in our profession there is no abler man than
you. Won't you step in?"

JIMMY CHRISTOPHER searched the woman's dark
eyes intently, the grimness of his gaze masked by the disarm-
ing warmth of his smile. "Permit me," he said, "to offer you my
own car. It is just ahead. In it, I am sure, we will be able to talk
more privately."

"Thank you."

"But first—"

Operator 5 stepped back; his quick signal brought Diane Elliot to his side. As he gestured her into the taxi his terse whisper was: "Search her, Di—and look sharp!" He closed the door upon the girl, stepped away, and nodded to bring Tim Donovan from the far side of the taxi.

"Jimmy, she told the driver to go to the Falker Building in Times Square!"

"Good work, Tim! You're coming with us. Watch that woman every second, old-timer—watch her! Don't think of her as the polished beautiful, utterly bewitching creature she is. Think of her as the most dangerous spy who ever lived, the greatest threat against the United States today. Don't trust any move she makes or any word she utters!"

The boy's eyes widened. "Sure, Jimmy!" and he hurried through the fluttering flakes to the roadster.

The door of the taxi clacked open. Diane Elliot ducked out; Radi Havara followed immediately.

"Nothing, Jimmy," Diane reported quickly.

The dark woman laughed again—a low, musical note. "I

might have assured you, Mr. Christopher," she said quietly, "that I am quite unarmed."

Operator 5 bowed once more. "I beg your pardon," he smiled, "for neglecting to ask."

He took Radi Havara's arm. To Diane he said quietly: "Please telephone Dad, Di. Ask him to relay to Z-7 that Miss Havara is occupying Rooms 1521 and 1522 at this hotel. I want them guarded—but not entered!—until I return. Until the men arrive, please keep an eye on them yourself—and then you're through."

"Until you return?" Radi Havara asked the question quite casually. "Are you sure, Mr. Christopher, that you will return?"

The very softness of her voice sent a twinge of coldness down Jimmy Christopher's spine. He glanced aside to see the color fading from Diane Elliot's cheeks. He looked into the deep darkness of Radi Havara's eyes as he answered: "I assure you that I will make every effort to return here—soon."

He escorted her toward the roadster. Tim Donovan opened the door for them; he slipped to the seat at the woman's side as Operator 5 took the wheel. The boy peered in unconcealed fascination at Radi Havara's beautiful face, and she smiled in return.

"I am quite delighted," she said, "that I have also the pleasure of meeting Tim Donovan tonight."

The boy's eyes widened with wonder, Jimmy Christopher made no answer until he had U-turned the car. Driving southward over the tire-marked lane of white, he smiled slowly.

"Tim is as delighted, I assure you, Miss Havara, to meet you—and amazed that you know him."

"Of course I know him. He is your closest friend and unofficial assistant. He helped you invaluably in the repulsion of the Shreckite invasion, in the saving of Alaska from the Asiatic hordes of Genghis Dhak, and in suppressing the danger of the New Populists.* You are fortunate, Mr. Christopher, to have such an able helper."

"Your sources of information, Miss Havara," Jimmy Christopher answered suavely, "are apparently completely trustworthy." "I ASSURE you they are," the dark woman answered as the car swung into a cross street. "There are not many points concerning you and your service, Mr. Christopher, of which I am uninformed. It is no secret to me that you are considered the ace undercover agent of your government. You are, I know, an honored graduate of the world-famous *Salle d'Armes* of Scherevesky. You trained intensively in jiu-jitsu under Kashawatska Hoia of Tokyo, who instructs the Heavenly Protectors of His Imperial Highness the Emperor of Japan. In addition, you are a skilled wrestler and boxer, a chemist, an expert in radio engineering, an amateur magician of great skill, and you are without peer in the field of deciphering code messages. Knowing this, I am sincerely honored by your attention tonight."

"Let us not argue," Operator 5 answered, "about my alleged talents. I am quite as well aware of your accomplishments as you are of mine. You are too young to have been active during the World War, but you have demonstrated your ability in the

* AUTHOR'S NOTE: Radi Havara is referring to the exploits of Operator 5 narrated under the titles of "Invasion of the Dark Legions," "The Green Death Mists," and "Legions of Starvation."

later espionage systems which are far more complex and far more dangerous. I compliment you when I confess that we have been utterly unable to learn which nation you are serving at the moment."

"Forgive me," Radi Havara smiled, "if I do not enlighten you on that point."

"Of course. But I must point out the chief reason for my interest in you tonight. It is merely that, while the activities of the United States Intelligence are confined strictly to defensive measures, your present work is destructive in the extreme."

"Destructive?"

"Destructive," Operator 5 affirmed, "of men's integrity—of men's lives—of the security of nations. Therefore I am obliged to hold you in custody on charges of, I regret to say, operating as an agent of a foreign government without having presented your credentials to the State Department—and of murder."

The dark woman was silent as the car turned and hummed southward again; then, very softly, she said: "I realize, of course, that there is but one penalty for failure in my work—the penalty of death."

"You are quite ready," Operator 5 asked gently, "to accept that penalty?"

"To accept it—and to inflict it."

Operator 5's dark eyes flashed to Radi Havara's face. For the first time her mask dropped; for an instant he glimpsed unmistakably the cruel ruthlessness, the merciless cunning of the woman. Her few, direct words were a horror-fraught threat that tightened Jimmy Christopher's hands on the wheel, that snapped his nerves to a tighter pitch of wary alertness.

"I believe," he said quietly, swinging the roadster to the curb, "that we have reached our destination."

He stepped out as Tim Donovan slipped the door open. He offered his hand to assist Radi Havara, and her cool slender fingers tightened on his. They straightened to gaze at a doorway—a shabby, unpainted entrance—above which peeled words read: *Falker Building*.

AROUND THEM buzzed the after-theater activity of Times Square. Taxies, their chains clanking, were shuttling along the snow-lined streets. Thousands were thronging the sidewalks, men and women in costly evening clothes shouldering past tattered hangers-on. Newsboys were howling. From all around came the glare of lights, of flashing signs overlapping flashing signs, of theater marquees, of windows and headlights. Around the Times Building, a ribboned stream of words was flashing news dispatches:

FOURTH—DEAD—MAN—STABBED—IN—
HEART—DROPS—INTO—HERALD—SQUARE—
POLICE—BAFFLED

"But not," Radi Havara said softly, "the young man known as Operator 5."

Jimmy Christopher again took her arm. "Shall we go in?" he suggested. "I believe you are expected here."

The dark woman's answer was an enigmatic smile. Operator 5 escorted her to the drab doorway. It gave into a musty hall from which a bare flight of steps ascended. It was a characteristically outmoded structure lost in the garishness of Broadway; its doorway might be passed a thousand times without being noticed once. Its street-level was occupied by a pharmacy and another store selling cheap stockings and lingerie; its second floor was dark, except for a yellow bulb burning above the landing.

Operator 5's gesture directed Tim Donovan to follow as he mounted the flight at the woman's side. He peered at four doors opening into the dusty hall; he tried them rapidly, one after another, and found each unlocked. Behind them lay empty, littered offices. Jimmy Christopher again took the arm of Radi Havara.

"It seems," he said, "we go higher."

"I believe the third floor is the top," she answered quietly. "You need not fear an attack. The building is quite empty. There is no one else here. I assure you I am telling the truth."

"Then this is a cover-address for you?" Jimmy Christopher inquired. "Or perhaps you gave this address to the driver because you recognized me in the hotel and knew I was following."

"Neither, Mr. Christopher," the woman answered. "I came here tonight for a very special and rather unusual reason."

"Which is—?"

"That," Radi Havara answered, her voice again dropping to a whisper, "you will soon learn."

Operator 5 sensed a menace in the words, but he smiled and took the woman's arm again. He escorted her up the second flight, with Tim Donovan following anxiously. Once more a dim yellow bulb lighted the landing, and four doors gave into empty, dusty rooms.

In that at the rear, Jimmy Christopher paused, peering at a huge and ancient black safe which sat in one corner. The enamel had peeled from it; its surface had rusted. He twisted the handle and found it locked. He straightened, a smile playing upon his lips.

"Empty?" he asked of Radi Havara.

"Quite empty."

"I cannot doubt the word of a lady," Operator 5 answered with a bow, "but I am obliged to see for myself."

"By all means."

HE FLASHED a warning glance at the alert Irish lad, and bent over the corroded combination dial. It turned with difficulty, until a few revolutions loosened it. Sensitive fingertips barely touching the metal, his ear turned close, Operator 5 moved the dial slowly back and forth. As he worked the hum of Times Square droned into the room; but there was no rustle of movement from either Tim Donovan or the dark woman.

Faint impulses felt through the dial, faint clicks heard through the steel panel, told Operator 5 that he was reaching the last turn of the combination. A final fall of a tumbler, sensed rather than heard or felt, straightened him. He twisted at the handle; it responded. He braced to pull the weighty door open.

"Jimmy!" A swift rustle of cloth sounded as the boy's warning alarmed Operator 5. He whirled to see Radi Havara running through the doorway into the forward room. He sprang after Tim Donovan as the boy groped at the woman and was struck backward by a vicious, resounding slap across the eyes. He reached the sill as the door slammed shut, as a bolt slid into its socket.

Instantly Operator 5 whirled. His hand slipped to the automatic holstered at his arm-pit as he thrust out the opposite door into the corridor. He stopped short, but there was no sound—no movement. The woman, he knew, could not have reached the stairs so quickly; she must still be in the forward room. He strode swiftly toward it and thrust the door wide.

The room was empty. Tim Donovan slid through the door behind Operator 5. He stopped, eyes rounded, amazed. He blurted: "Gee, Jimmy! She couldn't've got out—but where is she?"

"*That* door."

It was, apparently, the door of a closet, set in the side wall. The dust powdered on the floor in front of it had been undisturbed at Operator 5's first entrance; he had, for that reason, not touched it; but now small footsteps marked it, and the knob was wiped clean. He gestured a warning for Tim to stay back; he flattened to the wall beside it, reached out, twisted the knob. His thrust flung the door wide....

No movement, no sound came through it. Jimmy Christopher turned to peer into—emptiness. A few shelves inside were littered with paper. There was no piece of furniture. But, on the floor there were footprints—prints leading straight beneath the wall at the rear! No attempt had been made to disguise the fact that that wall had been broken out and a new section installed on a framework of angle-iron. A secret way out!

Operator 5 thrust at the new rectangle of bricks—and they yielded! Alertly he stepped through, upon a roof level with the lower edge of the door. The glare of Times Square shown upon the flat surface—upon fresh tracks in the snow, crossing to a skylight. A frame lay open. Operator 5 leaped to it, peered down—and sprang back as he sensed a warning movement below.

Three sharp clicks sounded. Into them resounded three breathy reports so muffled that they were almost swallowed in the clatter of Times Square. Past Jimmy Christopher's head, three bullets hissed venomously.

"Back, Tim!" he commanded as the Irish lad ran close. "Silenced rifle down there!"

"Gee, Jimmy! She's getting away!"

OPERATOR 5 whirled to the cornice; he looked down upon a sidewalk teeming with the after-theater crowds. In that human ambush any fugitive might become lost in a few seconds. That Radi Havara had already slipped from the building and into the swarm seemed certain. Jimmy Christopher turned back quickly; he tensed to spring through the door in the wall; abruptly, he paused.

His dark eyes turned upward. He stood rigid, listening. Beside him, Tim Donovan also came to a sudden standstill, also lifted his eyes into the snow-laden air. "Gee, Jimmy—what's that?"

It was a wail—a prolonged, ear-drilling scream that shrilled out of the heavens with swiftly increasing volume. It penetrated all the muffled rumble of Times Square. It rasped the nerves and pierced the brain with its steadily rising pitch. The continuous scream rose ever higher, penetrating from the black heights of the zenith, echoing from the buildings,—a horrible banshee cry. It stilled the busy rustle of Times Square and brought a hush of horror.

Jimmy Christopher glanced at the glowing dial of his wrist-watch. The last seconds before midnight were ticking away. The cryptic words of the perfumed message he had found on J-4's dead body—*Time first midnight*—flashed mockingly in his mind. And still, from the high reaches of the sky, the wail sounded, rising and swelling to an unearthly shriek.

"Jimmy!" Tim Donovan blurted, startled. "What is it?"

"Only one thing in the world makes that sound, Tim—only one!"

Seconds ticked away—each bringing the stroke of midnight closer—and the scream still shrilled!

"Inside, Tim—quick!" Jimmy Christopher swung the boy toward the door in the wall. He moved to follow through, paused. Still peering up into the sky, he saw a spark appear far above the swirl of the snow—a spark that brightened swiftly, that became a star falling. Behind it trailed a streak of incandescence as it lightninged downward—straight downward from directly overhead.

"In!"

Operator 5 sprang into the musty office. He unbolted the connecting door swiftly and gestured Tim Donovan into the rear office. Each movement was desperately fast as he seized the handle of the huge safe and braced to open it. All the while the horrible wail trembled through the air, growing unbearably loud, rising to a pitch that pained the ears.

Jimmy Christopher swung the slab of the safe open and peered into black emptiness. He whipped about to command, "Your belt, Tim—quick!" Eyes flashing darkly, he snatched the belt from the boy's hand and looped it with swift, deft fingers about the handle of the safe door. The whole room vibrated with the frightful sound wailing from the heavens.

"Get in there, Tim!"

Operator 5 gave the bewildered boy a push that stumbled him into the black interior of the safe. He whirled to follow, pulling on the belt. The heavy door swung as he crouched beside the boy—swung until it thudded upon the strip of leather, closed save for a fraction of an inch. Thick darkness surrounded them as they huddled there, and even into that steel-walled space, the piercing note drilled.

"Jimmy—!"

"A shell, Tim! A shell!"

The last second ticked away. Midnight! *It struck!*

THE FRIGHTFUL scream and the blinding streak of light ended in a blast of earth-shaking destruction.

In the very center of Times Square, the terrific concussion burst. Into the midst of carefree activity, havoc fell. One instant transformed the "crossroads of the world" into a scene of carnage and chaos.

At the focus of the square, a gargantuan crash sounded, followed instantly by a rending explosion that shot geysering flame high, spewing billowing fumes to the peaks of the buildings, flinging wreckage into suddenly roaring winds. The blinding flash vanished as swiftly as it had appeared while vapors rolled and terrified screams rang from the blackness that blanketed down. There followed the crashing of debris plummeting against the roofs and to the pavements, discording into a tinkling hail of shattered glass. Then a silence—stunned, awesome, complete....

The power of the concussion rocked the foundations of every building on the square. The horrified silence was broken after a few seconds by the dull thunder of collapsing walls. To the interior of the ancient Falker Building, the effects of the havoc penetrated.

Within the black confines of the steel-walled space, Operator 5 pulled hard on the strap which held the heavy door closed. The terrific jar of the first concussion had tossed the ponderous safe like a feather, but its thick sides had shielded Jimmy Christopher and Tim Donovan from the power of the blast. They felt the vault tilt as they huddled in utter darkness—as the hush closed down.

Operator 5 released the strap and thrust the door wide. He brought his torch into his hand as he eased out, and its beam

Tim Donovan

shot through air clouded with fumes and plaster dust. The light disclosed a ragged streak in the floor. The safe was leaning precariously toward the yawning gap. He grasped Tim Donovan's hand; he guided the boy to the burst door, and into the hallway.

Quiet snow was fluttering out of the night through the collapsed roof. The last wind of the explosion was soughing through the caved-in front wall. The building was trembling with a threat of further disintegration. Desperately, Operator 5 struggled over broken beams, urging the boy toward the head of the sagging stairs.

As they groped their way downward, a moan rose from the darkness of Times Square—a low, chorused wail of stunned grief. Jimmy Christopher and Tim Donovan fought through the broken doorway, into the fuming air of the street. In speechless consternation they peered upon a scene of incredible havoc.

In the center of Times Square, a great cavity lay open, rimmed by chunks of pavement, by up-curled trolley-tracks, by twisted ironwork. From the hollow hissed clouds of steam issuing from cracked distribution-mains. Around it lay scores of automobiles, thrown to their sides or upturned, crushed beneath falling sections of cement. A red light flickered high from the burning bodies of several taxies. In the street and on the sidewalks lay many sprawled, twisted forms—men and women struck down by the blast, unconscious, maimed, dying and dead....

OPERATOR 5 struggled through the milling crowd with Tim Donovan behind him. The shoes of the frantic living tramped over the lifeless bodies. A hysterical bedlam shook the air as fighting thousands clawed past other fighting thousands, thinking only of escaping from the scene of dreadful carnage. The open space was a whirlpool eddying with maddened humans, their clothing ripped, their faces and hands blotched with blood. And over all the scene, quiet snow settled through darkness.

Every sign within Times Square had ceased to flash. Every

window within sight was a ragged, black hole. Rooms and offices yawned open behind walls that had collapsed, flinging tons of masonry to the sidewalks. The front of every building was scarred and graven by flying fragments. Marquees had dropped over the entrances of theaters. Street-cars lay upturned or crushed on their tracks, terrorized scores of men and women trapped within them. In the blackness of the great cavity in the center of the square, two subway trains lay, a mass of wreckage on the fan of the tracks, marking the spot where hundreds had died at the bursting of the shell.

In the midst of the screaming confusion, in the center of the black chaos, Operator 5 stood with midnight-black eyes turning up and down the destruction-strewn streets which focused here. The horror of war had struck without warning into "the crossroads of the world."

High above the square, its great hands stopped by the blast of the explosion, the dark face of the clock on the Paramount tower indicated the hour when doom had come.

Midnight....

CHAPTER 3
ROBOTS IN FLIGHT

HIS FACE grim and dark-lined, Operator 5 fought through the maddened crowd with Tim Donovan at his side. Clawing mad hands snatched at him. His hat was knocked from his head and trampled into the reddened snow. Tim Donovan spun from his muffler as frantic hands gripped it, choking tight. Together, they fought their way to the curb where Jimmy Christopher had left his Diesel-engined roadster. It lay wrecked beneath a heap of bricks that had crushed down from the toppling wall of the Falker Building.

Desperately, he struggled to the cross-street, and shouldered along with the fleeing crowd. With Tim at his side, he slipped through the mob for blocks. When at last he was able to find an unengaged taxi, he signaled the Irish lad into it and ordered the driver: "Hotel Montblanc!"

The effects of the terrific explosion had struck a spell of horror across all of Manhattan. Along every street, groups of people were rushing from the center of destruction. Operator 5 sat tensely, saying nothing, while his cab shuttled eastward. The news of the blast had spread like wildfire; as he shouldered out with Tim, questions came at him from all sides. Lips pressed tight, he hurried with the boy into the foyer of the Montblanc. The elevator lifted them to the fifteenth floor. Tim strode with him down the corridor; they paused at the door numbered 1521. Operator 5 took the knob, found the way locked. He was bringing a pack of keys from his pocket when a click sounded behind him.

He turned quickly to see a door on the opposite side of the corridor closing. He knocked on it. Immediately it opened, and a quiet mannered man drew back to let Operator 5 and Tim Donovan step through. The door swung shut again.

Operator 5 asked: "You're from M-11?"

"Yes. I'm R-8. You're the first who's come to the suite across the way since I started watching it."

"You've made sure nobody knows you're keeping it under observation?"

"Perfectly sure."

"The key, then. Keep out of sight until I leave. Nab anyone who goes in after that. Those rooms were used by Radi Havara, but it's certain she'll never come back to them."

"Yes, sir!"

Operator 5 crossed the corridor. The key admitted him into a tastefully furnished sitting-room. An air of coldness about it convinced him that the woman espionage agent had not occupied it long. The adjoining bedroom showed few signs of occupancy. There were cosmetics on the dresser, a trim suit hanging in the closet above a pair of black oxfords; an almost empty suitcase. The desk had apparently not been used.

Jimmy Christopher began a systematic search. He removed pictures and mirrors from the wall and inspected their backs; he examined the lamps, the wainscoting, the mattress and the pillows of the bed. He inspected even the tiling in the bathroom, and even the edges of the carpet for any indication that a section might have been pried up. It was not until he examined the windows that his search was rewarded.

WHEN HE drew down the blind in the bedroom, a sheet of paper uncurled from the rod. Quickly he brought it under a light to examine it. He smiled tightly as he straightened.

"Apparently," he remarked to Tim Donovan, "a perfectly innocent personal letter dealing with trivialities. But no one takes such pains to hide a trivial letter." The boy raised a hand quickly, in warning. "Jimmy! Sounds like somebody at the door!"

47

Operator 5's eyes narrowed as he listened. He agreed at once, "You're right, Tim."

He folded the letter quickly, thrust it into his pocket as he stepped into the living room. The entrance stood at the end of a short passage from which doors opened into a closet and a bath. Jimmy Christopher signaled Tim Donovan into the closet. He followed, closed the door, and slid his hand warily to his automatic as a key clicked in the outer lock.

Another click signaled the closing of the door. Quiet footfalls passed. They paused beyond in the sitting-room. A man's voice called quietly:

"Nadaya!"

Jimmy Christopher recognized the name as one of Radi Havara's known aliases. Very quietly, he twisted the catch of the closet door. He glided out, automatic leveled, toward a tall, lean man whose back was turned to peer into the bedroom. He asked softly: "You're looking for someone?"

The tall man whipped around. His sharp, lean face flashed pale at sight of the leveled weapon. His deep-set eyes, a faded brown, darkened under lowering lids. In a burst of breath he asked: "Who are you?"

"That," Operator 5 retorted, "is the precise question I was about to put. You may answer it now, or you may prefer to wait until you have been taken into custody."

"Into—!" The lean man straightened quickly. "You're not—"

"A friend, perhaps a co-worker of the woman you call Nadaya? Scarcely." Operator 5's slow smile came. "But you, of course, are."

The lean man's words snapped. "What're you doing here? What do you want? Can't I step in to visit a friend without—?"

Operator 5 cut in quickly: "Let's not bluff, V-44."

The thin face reddened, then whitened again. No change of Operator 5's expression betrayed the satisfaction he felt at knowing his random shot had told. He gestured to Tim Donovan.

"Take his gun, old-timer. We had best not waste time here. We will learn soon enough why an Englishman is working with the espionage of a nation foreign to him and to us."

Again the tall man started. He allowed the Irish lad to probe beneath his coat and remove a small automatic. He made a gesture of resignation.

"Who you are and what you intend to do to me," he said tensely, "I do not know—but I'm sure you know a great deal about me. My—my activities have been kept from my wife— do you understand? She knows nothing about them. If you take me with you, my absence will worry her. I ask your permission to telephone her and give her some excuse that will cover—"

"As you like."

The lean man turned slowly toward the instrument on the desk. He fumbled it as he raised; the receiver dropped to the length of the cord. He reached toward it as he turned—turned swiftly. The heavy receiver became a black streak flying with vicious power toward Operator 5's gun-hand.

JIMMY CHRISTOPHER stepped back swiftly as the flying receiver flashed past, striking Tim Donovan's head. The boy gave a startled moaning gasp, sprawled sideward as the lean man leaped. The lean man struck at Operator 5 savagely with the telephone as his cudgel. Jimmy Christopher's finger was tight on the trigger, but he did not fire. A jerk of his head and he avoided the slashing blow; a quick side-step, and he drove stiffened fingers to the side of the tall man's neck.

Breath burst from the man's lungs as he toppled. Jimmy Christopher followed with a quick step as he dropped his automatic into his pocket. He snatched at the other man's lapels; he brought his thumbs to bear forcibly against two nerve-centers in the throat. Quietly, the lean man dropped from his grasp—unconscious.

The effects of the jiu-jitsu blow would keep him unconscious, Operator 5 knew, the better part of an hour. He spun to seize Tim Donovan's arm as the boy struggled up. "I'm all right, Jimmy! Gee, I thought I was going out for a minute—but I'm all right!"

"Good boy, Tim! Watch him! I—"

Jimmy Christopher broke off, listening. He stepped to the window, flung it wide. While Tim Donovan leveled the visitor's automatic at him, Operator 5 leaned out into the falling snow. From far away, muffled and indistinct, came a single, rolling boom of thunder.

A moment later, another sounded; a third followed. Operator 5 turned from the window with eyelids lowered thoughtfully. He stepped to the telephone; he gave the hotel operator a secret number. When his connection clicked through, he exchanged signals with a communications-man at Headquarters M-11.

"Mr. Quintus calling Mr. Sept."

Almost immediately the crisp, deep voice of Z-7, Chief of the United States Intelligence, rang over the wire.

Immediately, Operator 5 directed: "An ambulance at once to the Montblanc, Room 1521. A friend of mine is here, very ill—do you understand? Please send—"

"Yes, yes! It will be done—but wait! I've just had a flash from MF! It is being attacked—bombed—by a squadron of airplanes!"

Jimmy Christopher's hands whitened on the instrument. The symbol MF he knew, signified the most important army air base on the Eastern center—Mitchell Field. The voice of Z-7 rang imperatively again over the wire:

"We have been caught utterly unprepared! The bombardment of the enemy planes is shifting now toward Fort Hancock on Sandy Hook! Everything we have been able to do so far has not stopped them! It means that New York will be bombed next unless—"

"I'm leaving at once," Operator 5 interrupted swiftly, "for Mitchell Field!"

OUT OF the darkness that lay over the sea beyond New York, the whipping roar of airplanes sounded.

The great tarmac of Mitchell Field, on Long Island, lay blanketed by snow and shrouded by the night. The whiteness of the ground was gashed by the tracks of the trucks and tail-skids of combat-planes hastily warmed and launched into the heavens. No gleam of light shown from any beacon or any window on the field; at the first whine of a dropping bomb, at the first blasting explosion, every light had blinked out. Now a line of combat-crates sat in the gloom, their props slashing the air, their pilots waiting tensely in the pits for the order that would swoop the war birds into the sky.

Behind the planes yawned black cavities dug by the bursting bombs. The windows of the operations-office and the barracks were shattered. An ambulance was backed to the hospital and still forms on litters were being carried through a dark doorway. On the field, peering into the humming sky, grim-faced officers stood, stunned by the sudden devastation of the attack.

Swiftly, from the guarded gate, a sedan with dead headlights streaked across the field with snow flying from its tire-chains. Before it braked to a stop, a taxi swung in to follow. From the first alighted a hard-faced man garbed in a great gray coat, his gleaming black eyes shaded by the low-pulled brim of a black felt hat. Officers hurried toward him as he turned toward the taxi.

From the cab, Operator 5 descended quickly, Tim Donovan following anxiously. They hastened to the gray-clad man as officers shouldered around them. Before either spoke, they listened to the turmoil in the sky—to snarling motors sounding far above, to dull booming concussions that echoed out of the dark distance.

"Those are the anti-aircraft batteries at Fort Hancock firing at the enemy planes!" The straight-backed, ruddy-faced officer who spoke was Major Clark Acheson, Acting Commander of the air-base. "We've ordered our fliers to attack from the west to keep those crates from reaching New York! So far we haven't dropped one of them!"

The gray-clad man turned smoldering black eyes upon

Operator 5. His identity, like that of Jimmy Christopher, was unknown to most of the officers present. Secrecy cloaked their work alike. The ebon-eyed man was Z-7. He declared grimly: "This attack has caught us completely unawares. Half an hour ago, there was no hint of it. Now there's a full squadron of enemy planes hammering at our defenses with H.E. bombs...." His gaze snapped at Major Acheson. "In God's name, where did those planes come from?"

"We don't know! They struck at us out of nowhere, without warning! Three bombs dropped before we could get our planes into the air. The Squadron leader has radioed us that there are no identifying marks on the planes. We're being attacked, and by God we don't know who's doing it!"

From the snow-swirled darkness, the drone of a motor was loudening. Somewhere above, a plane was spiraling about the field, dropping lower. There was still no sign of it when Z-7 demanded wrathfully:

"Those planes had to come from somewhere! It's certain that no enemy could have hidden them in this country without our knowing it. We keep a strict check on all planes produced that are of the combat type or that might be converted to war-time use—they couldn't have been built in this country. Certainly they couldn't have been smuggled in because, since the Shreck-ite invasion, we have guarded every possible way. I tell you—"

"**THE SHELL** that dropped into Times Square an hour ago must have been fired from a gun inside this country!" Major Acheson snapped. "Likewise, these planes must have been hidden somewhere near here in spite of your precautions!

53

Your men, sir, are not obliged to fight those planes—that might account for your carelessness!"

Z-7's eyes gleamed with the diamond-brightness of anger. "Very well!" he snapped. "Fight those planes down! Keep them from reaching Fort Totten and dropping bombs into Manhattan!"

"Fight them? By God, sir, we are fighting them!" Major Acheson thundered. "We have them out-numbered at this moment! Our second flight is ready to takeoff the instant the enemy planes press inward, if they manage to do it! We're doing everything possible to knock those crates down. I'm damned if I can explain why none of them has fallen!"

Operator 5 spoke quietly. "None of them has fallen because those planes are completely armored, and because they are being controlled by—"

The thunderous roar of the descending airplane drowned out his soft words. Out of the darkness of the sky it swooped. It dipped toward the white ground while the pilot peered intently overside. He zoomed, banked, drove low again, swept his trucks close above the line of waiting planes, and slashed into the snow.

Operator 5, Tim Donovan and Z-7 hurried with the stunned officers toward it. The pilot scrambled from its pit the instant the brakes held, began a crazy run across the field. He brought up breathless before the officers. He made a bewildered gesture toward his plane before he could summon his voice.

The combat ship was peppered with black holes bored through its fuselage by hailing slugs. Its wings were ribboned.

From its motor-housing, oil was dripping. It had met a terrific machine-gun attack in the sky.

"God—we can't drop 'em! We can't touch 'em! They keep flying—flying!"

Major Acheson began: "What the devil do you mean, sir—"

"They're ghost ships! Ghost ships!"

"Are you crazy! Those planes have dropped—"

"There are no men in the pits!"

The blurted words brought silence. Officers peered into the pilot's greasy, fear-twisted face. Operator 5 watched him intently as he gestured again, groping for words to make believable the incredibility of what he had seen in the sky.

"I got one of 'em dead on my sights! I opened my guns and let it have a long burst! I saw the tracers hitting it—but nothing happened! It didn't even bank away! It wasn't even hurt! It kept flying—while I emptied a drum at it! It dropped a bomb while I was chasing it! Then I saw there wasn't any pilot in the pit!"

"By God!" Major Acheson roared. "Man, you're mad!"

"Mad, am I?" the lieutenant choked. "You fly up there and see for yourself! You take a look into those pits! There's not a man in any of 'em! They're all flying empty! They're all roaring around, dropping bombs, and bullets can't stop 'em! Armored— sure, I know that! Armored even so the motors can't be conked! But there isn't a pilot at any of the controls. There's not a man in those pits!"

Again appalled silence settled over the group on the snowy field.

"We can't stop 'em! Send up a thousand planes to load bullets into 'em, and we won't be able to stop 'em! There's a couple of crates up higher that keep slamming slugs into us while we try to drop those bombers and it's no use! Throw the whole army air corps up there to fight if you want. They won't be able to knock down a single one of those damned crates!"

MAJOR ACHESON glared. The stricken pilot peered horrified into the sky. Until that moment no one had noticed that the stiff fingers of his right hand were dripping blood, that

RADI HAVARA

his sleeve was reddened and bullet-torn. Z-7's black eyes shifted haggardly as Operator 5 stepped briskly toward the Acting Commander.

"I wish to be allowed to take one of your planes up immediately, sir."

"What? You? Why—"

"In addition, I suggest urgent orders. Direct your men to bring from the barracks, immediately, every available pillow. Load your second flight planes with as many of those pillows as can be crammed into the pits. Call—"

"Pillows?" Major Acheson grated. "What the devil are you talking about? With enemy bombers flying above us, you—"

"Those pillows," Operator 5 interrupted crisply, "are to be used for the purpose of knocking the enemy bombers from the sky."

Acheson roared: *"What?"* His neck became corded with throbbing veins. He blurted: "Crazy! You're all—!"

"Unless you wish the enemy bombers to break through and hit New York—follow those orders!" Jimmy Christopher snapped, his eyes glinting. "Call down your first flight at once! Send all your men off this field—along the roads and into the homes—to confiscate every pillow that can be found! Send your first flight back up, after the second, with all the pillows they can carry! At once, sir!"

Acheson growled: "You're talking like a lunatic—fighting bombers with pillows! And by God, sir, I don't know you and I'm not taking orders from you!"

Z-7's hand tightened about the Acting Commander's wrist. "The General Staff," he declared, "in past emergencies, has followed without question strategies and tactics outlined by this young man. You will do well to obey him. He is Operator 5."

"Operator—5!" The Major stared incredulously. "By God, how was I to know? Operator 5, eh? I beg your pardon, gentlemen! I—"

"Issue those orders at once, Major!" Jimmy Christopher insisted. "I'll follow them up from the air!"

He broke into a run and the amazed officers stared after him. Tim Donovan trotted beside him to the wing of the first two-seater in the line. One of the officers followed to authorize Jimmy Christopher's orders—orders that brought the pilot of the plane scrambling from the pit. Operator 5 drew on helmet and goggles quickly; he legged across the cowling to the controls.

From the distance the dull thunder of the anti-aircraft batteries was still thumping; from above, the whipping drone of the battling planes continued.

Operator 5 thrust the throttle wide. He glanced back to see Tim Donovan clambering madly over the cowling of the rear pit, crowding down beside the startled observer. There was no time to warn the boy to stay back. Jimmy Christopher threw off the brakes and sent the plane driving swiftly across the field. A snowy storm followed in his wake as he sent the crate driving into a climb.

He glanced down to see dim dark figures hurrying from the barracks, their arms tightened about masses of pillows. Men were already cramming the soft bags into the pits of waiting planes. The incongruous sight made Jimmy Christopher's lips tighten wryly. He glanced back again to see Tim Donovan grimly hanging to the cowling, head bowed against the cyclonic wind. Then he sent the plane driving high.

He snapped on the radio equipment of the plane, plugged into the pin-jacks the rips of the cord connecting with the ear-'phones affixed within his helmet. He lowered over his head a spider that suspended a microphone before his lips. The rush of the carrier-wave sounded in the 'phones as the tubes reached operating heat.

"Calling MF! Ask Major Acheson to order his flight up as soon as they are loaded with all the pillows they can carry! The first flight is to come down at once for a second load! In the meantime, order the second to climb to a position above the enemy bombers!"

"Major Acheson is carrying out your orders!" a voice sang from the field that was lost in the darkness below. "Flight B is taking off now!"

Still higher Operator 5 flung his plane, while snow whipped past the windshield, torn in the turmoil of the propeller. The ground was a blear of scattered points of light shining through the haze of the snowfall. Within the pattern of them lay a black gap—the water of the bay. Operator 5 drove above it, into that tumultuous region of the air where battle birds were fighting.

Below, a splash of light appeared, instantly to disappear, followed in a moment by a thunderous burst that penetrated the drone of the motors. Another bomb had been dropped; destruction had again struck from the sky. Immediately flaring flashes appeared—the flames of anti-aircraft batteries firing from Fort Hancock. In the distance gleamed the halo of light that beaconed Manhattan.

In the sky above the bay, black-winged forms were flitting—enemy bombers bearing toward the objective of the metropolis.

CHAPTER 4
TERROR IN TWELVES

S WIFTLY THROUGH the sifting snow, Jimmy Christopher spiraled his plane until he hovered high above the
strife-torn air. The dim shine of light from the widespread city
enabled him to follow the great black bats of war. He circled
slowly, watching a ragged formation drawing away into the
darkness and another banking beyond the tip of Manhattan.

The first flock passed beneath him. It was, he knew, Flight A
from Mitchell Field, returning to its base under radioed orders
from the Acting Commander. The second bevy, spiraling with
slow confidence below the city, was the mysterious enemy
bombers. In a moment, out of the swirling depths of the sky, a
third formation appeared—Flight B.

They swooped below, driving toward the enemy crates. The
glow was enough to show Operator 5 their pits packed with
pillows—pillows thrust down at the sides of the pilots, pillows
crammed tight about the observers. Immediately he called again
into the microphone:

"Calling MF! Relay orders to the pilots and observers of
Flight B! As they proceed, they are to cut or tear open their
pillows and hold them ready. Once in position above the enemy
bombers, they are to shake the feathers into the air. Flight A is
to follow the same orders as quickly as possible!"

There was a puzzled hesitation before the answer came
through the ether: "Orders being relayed!"

Operator 5 sent his crate droning toward the bombers. They

It was cunningly disguised airplane carrier—of the nation

which led a double attack upon New York that night!

had circled as though in preparation for a coördinated attack. Now they were leveling, turning their noses toward the shine of New York, dressing off in a straight flight toward their objective. The light disclosed glistening bombs still resting in the racks, waiting to be tripped. And above them, at top speed. Flight B from Mitchell Field began to mass.

63

From his high position, Jimmy Christopher peered down upon the strange scene. Far below, black enemy planes were driving wing to wing toward Manhattan—planes that were empty-pitted, flying without the guidance of human hands at the controls! Above them, the gray army crates were circling, pilots and observers working frantically with their cargoes of pillows. Both flocks were swarming into the glow of Manhattan lights—closer to the point where the remaining loads of enemy bombs obviously were to be dropped to spread red ruin.

Operator 5 snapped into his microphone: "Empty the pillows now! *Now!*"

Through the ether, to the field and back his words lightninged. His orders were obeyed immediately. United States army flyers shook ripped-open pillows and masses of fluttering white clouded into the air to mingle with the snow. As the scores of pillows were emptied, feathers fluffed into a nebulous mass that blanketed down upon the enemy bombers. Thicker and thicker the white cloud grew, swelling, rolling, torn by the slipstreams of the planes, engulfing the black, winged attackers in its midst.

Into Operator 5's 'phones rang: "Flight A taking-off. Flight B reports all pillows emptied. Wait! The B Flight leader is reporting! Several of the enemy planes are going down. The entire formation of bombers is having trouble. For God's sake, we're stopping them!"

"Instruct A Flight to follow as fast as possible!" Jimmy Christopher ordered quickly. "Same procedure! Pillows to be emptied directly above—"

"Good Lord—are you a wizard?" the officer on Mitchell Field blurted. "Those planes are all dropping! They're going to fall into the bay before they reach Manhattan! Some of them are releasing bombs, but the charges are hitting the water and doing no damage! Can you confirm those reports?"

PEERING OVERSIDE grimly, Jimmy Christopher watched the black enemy formation wavering, scattering, staggering deeper into the spreading blackness of the bay. Far beneath them, splashes of light flickered, and into the zenith rumbled the thunder of the bomb explosions. Steadily lower the enemy crates were being forced, while the air clouded thick with drifting down.

"I confirm the reports—fully!" Jimmy Christopher chuckled into the microphone. "This way of knocking planes from the sky is scarcely supernatural. You've been trained in the use of armament—you think in terms of guns and explosives. Those enemy crates are armored against your bullets and they carry no pilots to be killed—but feathers have penetrated to vital points that bullets cannot reach."

"But, good Lord! How—?"

"It is, simply that the feathers have been sucked into the air-intakes of the motors." Jimmy Christopher answered. "The intakes have become clogged. Lacking air, the engines cannot run. It's as simple as that!"

From below sounded an amazed exclamation: "I'll be damned!"

Still peering overside, Jimmy Christopher added: "All the planes are going down! Three have hit the water and are sinking.

The bombing attack on New York has been stopped. A flight can be instructed to save its pillows!"

Over the air Major Acheson's gruff voice growled. "By God, Operator 5, I offer you my compliments! Dropping a flight of bombers with nothing more deadly than eiderdown! Words fail me! I'll consider it an honor, sir, to shake your hand if—"

From the rear pit Tim Donovan cried sharply: "Jimmy, look out! Look—!" Sudden, vicious, slashing power struck the words away.

Out of the night above Operator 5, an onslaught of slugs hammered. The ominous *brrrrrt* of a machine gun stuttered from the higher air as spotted flame flashed and black wings swooped low. The burst of fire passed directly beside Jimmy Christopher, to pelt into the black box of the radio equipment, destroying it instantly. Swiftly, overhead, a pursuit whipped about to gain a position for a renewed attack!

Jimmy Christopher wrenched at the controls and sent the two-seater roaring through a roll even before he glimpsed the black wings of the attacking plane. He righted himself to find two crates howling down upon him. He pulled into a sharp zoom as they thundered toward his tail; he Immelmanned and spun vertical-winged to throw his nose in the direction of one of the swooping vultures. He hunched behind the ring-sights of his guns; and as motion flashed on the crossed wires he pressed the Bowden-trips.

The burst chopped across the wings of the black plane; hacked straight across the pit. At once the crate leaned upon one stitched wing and swooped into a spiral that tightened swiftly into a spin.

Operator 5 twisted to see the other plane howling down from above. He dived past the fluttering crate that was doomed to destruction in the water below. As he straightened a withering blast struck from the higher air, slashing across his wings.

The burst damaged Operator 5's crate only slightly, but his instant decision upon a subterfuge sent him downward in a ragged dive. He nudged his controls to imitate the faltering of a ship whose pilot is wounded; he allowed the ship to slip into a spin and gyrated swiftly downward through the beating snow. When he was certain that he had passed beyond sight of the attacking crate, he kicked the rudders in the opposite direction, checked the spin, and thrust the stick far forward. The gyrations slowed, and when the crate suddenly swooped level, Jimmy Christopher was shuttling low above black water.

He circled slowly, peering up, sensing the presence of the other plane above him. He heard Tim's anxious call: "Jimmy, did he get you?" and turned quickly to smile his reassurance to the anxious boy. He hovered low above the bay until he glimpsed black wings flitting above—the enemy plane darting toward the open sea.

USING HIS engine as little as possible, mushing into glides and pulling up again, Operator 5 kept that plane in sight. The darkness grew thicker; a screen of snow shielded him from the pilot above. The black crate coursed steadily seaward. When, finally, it banked quickly, Operator 5 let his plane glide, watched alertly.

On the water, riding the waves, loomed the black hulk of a freighter, its lanterns twinkling through the snowfall. It was, as far as Operator 5 could discern in the gloom, different in no respect from thousands of other merchant ships that plied the seven seas. Yet now the enemy bomber was spiraling low around it. The plane threw down its retractable floats easily, dropped to the inky water.

Operator 5 hovered in the air at a distance, watching in amazement. He saw a wide section of the ship's hull open—a great leaf lowered on chains, its hinged edge almost at the water level. Like a drawbridge, it swung down to a slight slope while the convertible bomber bobbed toward it. Men put out in a small boat, dragging a cable which they hooked to the landing-gear of the plane. A winch tightened, drawing the ship up on the sloping leaf.

Again rolling on its wheels, the crate was towed inward. The chains tightened to raise the hinged section. The broad opening closed slowly and the interior lights blinked out. Again, within the space of a few moments, the ship became to all appearances an ordinary freighter.

Operator 5 smiled wryly. He had learned part of the secret of the cunningly-disguised airplane-carrier which had launched a double attack upon New York that night.

He swung closer in an attempt to discern its approximate position and its name. He circled once, slowly. He was just leveling off when a brilliant white beam blazed from the craft's deck—the shaft of a powerful searchlight that swung in agitated search of Operator 5's plane.

"Jimmy!" Tim Donovan called in anguish. "They heard you! Look out for—"

The crash of an anti-aircraft gun sounded its own warning. The shell streaked high to burst with a hollow roar that sent fragments of shrapnel spraying across the sky. Close to Operator 5's crate, the charge roared its power while the searching beam swung. Swiftly Jimmy Christopher banked; at full power he roared low over the black water.

Behind him the guns crashed again; above him, the shells shattered. The white beam swung low, slashing through the thick snow toward him. He rocked from wing to wing, evading the light; he sped far beyond the reach of any gun the disguised airplane conveyor might carry. His radio equipment was useless; he could warn Mitchell Field now of this enemy craft in only one way—personally. At the limit of its power, his engine roared, swooping him through the flicking snow.

Then suddenly, three muffled explosions, echoing dully across the water, turned Operator 5's head quickly toward the disguised freighter. He glimpsed flashing flame through the snowfall, heard again the ominous rumble of powerful reports. He banked swiftly, his power plant still revving at its highest, howled back through the night.

When he swung into another circle, it was to gaze down upon flames flickering across a deck already awash. Black water was flooding wildly across a broken ship—a ship swiftly sinking....

Operator 5 circled, peering down grimly, until it plunged beneath the surface. Into the depths of the bay, black as doom, disappeared steamer and plane and men—men who, destroying an engine of war, had destroyed themselves....

THE WINDOWS of Marielle's establishment were dark

and curtained that early morning hour, when Operator 5, Z-7, and Tim Donovan code-worded their way into the secret headquarters. They stepped through a soundproofed door, into the inner office of the chief, and an atmosphere of feverish activity.

Immediately the communications-room opened; the clattering sounds of teletypes invaded the office as the chief-dispatcher hurried with reports to Z-7's desk.

"A message direct from the White House, just off the wire," he exclaimed. "The President is requesting a full, confidential report."

"Please advise the President that we will wire the report shortly." Z-7's gaze turned grimly upon Jimmy Christopher. "God knows I can tell him very little. I need the information you have correlated, Operator 5. This is the first opportunity we'd had to discuss it; let's waste no time!"

"First, sir—!" The dispatcher gestured anxiously. "Major-General Newcomb is telephoning from Washington, asking to speak with Operator 5."

"Connect him with this desk," Jimmy Christopher directed, taking up the instrument.

The man whose voice burst over the line was that of the chief of the United States army air corps. "Operator 5," he began hastily, "I have been talking with Major Acheson. What he tells me sounds like the ravings of a lunatic. What the devil has happened? How the devil will we be able to fight ships that—"

"One moment, General Newcomb," Jimmy Christopher broke in. "Major Acheson's report is startling, I know, but every word of it is true. The planes that bombed us tonight were not

70

only armored—they were robot ships controlled entirely by radio impulses!"

"What?"

"Certainly! This should not be a great surprise to you, General Newcomb. We have already had reports from our agents in Europe that such planes have been built—the news has actually leaked through to the press."*

"I know that, but—good God, no one could have dreamed that they would be turned against us! Do you infer that tonight's attack was directed by French agents?"

"Not at all," Operator 5 answered quickly. "What I do mean is that since the secret of these radio-controlled planes has leaked out, another nation has built them and has used them against us. More than that, we may expect them to be used again!"

"But how the devil can we fight planes in which there are

---

* AUTHOR's NOTE: The Associated Press under date of August 3, 1934, distributed the following dispatch:

"Paris—An invention designed to enable airplanes to operate automatically, even in taking off and landing, has been acquired by the French Army after a year of tests at Istres Airport, it was learned today.

"The invention, the work of the four French engineers, is said to simplify piloting to an extent that would enable a child to operate a plane.

"All maneuvers in flying are said to be entirely automatic. The controls may be operated directly by push-buttons, or by means of radio impulses sent from a directing station which may be carried in another plane."

no pilots—planes that are armored against shell attacks? Our newest anti-aircraft guns were ineffective against them!" *

"CERTAINLY," OPERATOR 5 answered wryly, "we cannot depend upon feathers again to drop these planes, General Newcomb! There are two means of combating them. First, the controlling planes—which carry pilots who operate the radio-directors—must be located and shot down in case of a new attack. These always fly above the radio-controlled crates and they are able to direct ten or fifteen of them. A human factor is involved there and we must take advantage of it.

"Second, the source of the planes must be cut off. Those that tried to hit New York tonight came from an aircraft-carrier disguised as a freighter, stationed in the outer bay. Our Coast Guard cutters must be ordered at once to search for other ships that may have brought enemy airplanes close to our shores. A sharp watch must be maintained constantly otherwise we may certainly look for a renewed attack."

"Those means will be taken. By God, sir!" Major-General Newcomb exploded. "It's the devil's own work—fighting with robots—making an attack in which living men take almost no part!"

---

* AUTHOR'S NOTE: Major-General Newcomb is referring to a new gun with which the United States Army experimented during the last summer. It is a "stratospheric" weapon which ballistic experts believe will reach a vertical range of ten miles. It is equipped with special electrical altitude-finders, range-finders speed- and directions-indicators, and is one of the most efficient defense weapons in existence.

"What we have already experienced," Operator 5 declared grimly, "is only a hint of what will happen unless we can effectively use our means of counter-attack. It's entirely possible that gigantic swarms of planes might attack, bomb, and destroy our most vital defenses—a devastating attack controlled by no more than a handful of men!"

Jimmy Christopher turned from the telephone to find Z-7 peering at him haggardly. "That disguised airplane carrier, chief, was destroyed by the men aboard her as soon as they became certain that news of it would reach our Army Command. I couldn't identify it. The crew made sure that it would not provide us with a lead to more vital information, by sinking it. Orders must go out immediately, and our agents must concentrate on learning the nationality of that craft if possible."

Z-7's fist banged the desk. "Great Scott! New York attacked, and we don't know by what nation, or for what reason!"

He brought from a table a thick pack of newspapers still wet from the presses. Their front pages were blackened by banner headlines shouting the double disaster of the Times Square explosion and the aerial attack.

TIMES SQUARE ROCKED BY
TERRIFIC CONCUSSION!
HUNDREDS KILLED, THOUSANDS
INJURED BY BLAST!
CITY PARALYZED! MILLIONS IN
PROPERTY DAMAGE!
TIMES SQUARE EVACUATED,

GUARDED BY ARMY TROOPS!
RUINS SEARCHED FOR MISSING DEAD!
CITY TERRORIZED BY
MIDNIGHT DESTRUCTION!

"God—to what purpose?" Z-7 demanded dazedly. "Why was this attack directed against us—and by whom? The results are horrible, and yet it has accomplished no military advantage. Our defenses were not touched. A ghastly blow struck against civilians—*why?*"

Operator 5's darkened eyes turned upon the Washington chief. His right hand raised in an unconscious gesture. On the back of it a strange scar shone—a figure of black and white and gray shaped like a spread-winged American eagle. Its wings seemed to flex, as if straining for flight, as Jimmy Christopher's slender fingers toyed with a tiny object dangling from his watch-chain. It was a charm—a cunningly contrived skull-and-cross-bones of gold, its eyes jewels that flashed ruby-red.

"The real meaning of this attack, Chief, is hidden deeply in the intrigue of Radi Havara. The threat against us is all the more dangerous because we don't yet know the motive or the power behind it. We can't overlook a single chance of getting at the bottom of this case. We can't waste a moment. Orders, Chief!"

Z-7 TOUCHED a button on the desk as Operator 5 swung briskly to a typewriter. The chief dispatcher came from the communications-room in answer to the summons, and stood by alertly while Jimmy Christopher tapped the keys. He ripped a yellow sheet from the machine.

TO ALL INTELLIGENCE HEADQUARTERS: EVERY OPERATOR IS TO CONCENTRATE ON THESE ORDERS. OBJECT: TO DISCOVER IF A REPORT LIKE THAT OF A BIG GUN WAS HEARD ANYWHERE WITHIN THE COUNTRY A FEW SECONDS BEFORE MIDNIGHT LAST NIGHT. IF SUCH REPORT WAS HEARD, ITS LOCATION IS TO BE DETERMINED AS EXACTLY AND AS QUICKLY AS POSSIBLE.

Z-7 passed the order to the dispatcher, who hurried from the room. The Washington chief asked quickly:

"A big gun—located anywhere within the country? Do you believe that a piece of artillery of such range has been turned upon us? Is such a tremendous weapon possible?"

"Entirely possible, Chief! It's probably a gun incomparably greater in power than the 'Big Bertha' that the Germans used to shell Paris during the World War.* Since the war, develop-

---

* AUTHOR'S NOTE: The gun called "Big Bertha," named after Frau Bertha von Bohlen, the principal proprietor of the Krupp factor in which it was made, began shelling Paris from the forest of Saint-Gobain, near Coucy le Château, on March 23, 1918, and continued to fire every third day for 140 days, throwing shells into the city from a distance of 76 miles. On Good Friday, March 2, one of its shells struck the church of Saint-Gervais, killing and wounding 156 persons including women and children. It was a high velocity cannon, made by boring out a 15-inch naval gun and inserting a projecting tube of 21-centimeter caliber, which was rebored as it became worn. It had a muzzle velocity of 5,000 foot-seconds. The shells weighed

ments have greatly increased the range, accuracy, fire-power and mobility of artillery. There have been further important advances in methods of survey. It is my conviction, Chief, that the shell which hit New York last night was fired from a gun so big that beside it, 'Big Bertha' would seem comparatively puny!"

Again Operator 5 swung to the typewriter and wrote rapidly. Z-7's dark eyes sharpened at the supplementary order before he passed it into the hands of the dispatcher:

> TO HEADQUARTERS PHP:
> IMPERATIVE! ORDER MOST ABLE AGENTS TO UNDERTAKE IMMEDIATELY INVESTIGATION TO DETERMINE IF GUN OF UNPRECEDENTED RANGE WAS CONSTRUCTED IN ANY STEEL PLANT WITHIN THE U.S. REPORTS URGENT.

"But, Operator 5," Z-7 asked quickly, "shouldn't we restrict our investigation to a comparatively small area around New York—say a circle with a diameter of one hundred miles? Surely there are limitations on the range of artillery, which narrow its possible locations and—"

265 pounds and were fired at an elevation of 55 degrees. They reached thin air at a height of ten miles where little resistance to flight was offered; the greatest height of the trajectory was 24 miles. In connection with this gun, it is a little-known fact, that plans for its construction existed as long ago as 1888. In that year, a French spy visited Essen and brought back a copy of the original sketches. The gun was not built and used until thirty years after its construction was conceived.

"The limitations on the size and weight of artillery, Chief, are those of mobility, supply and signal communication. That is, the size of big guns is limited first of all by the difficulty of transportation, by the capacity of the rails over which they are to be moved. The limit of the great main roads of Europe, for instance, is thirty tons—sometimes as little as five—and in this country the limit is somewhat higher. But the gun which fired into Times Square last night has no such limitations.

"It must be anchored, hence the problem of mobility is removed. The difficulty of supply and signal communications have, I assure you, been eliminated. Therefore, we do not dare restrict our field of investigation to any small area. Keep in mind, Chief, that even the published data of the new German radio gun states that its range is at least two hundred miles."*

* AUTHOR'S NOTE: Operator 5 is referring to a significant news dispatch dated at Paris and published late last summer:

"It has been established to the satisfaction of French military authorities that the Germans have a new gun capable of shooting 200 miles. The projectile launched by the new big gun would mount so high that it will pass through the stratosphere. Two well-known German ballistic experts are quoted in secret information obtained by military officers as saying that the new cannon depends for its secondary motive power on a motor driving its projectile up by a series of explosions into the stratosphere. Once there, it is directed by wireless. The original impulse is given by an explosion of the usual sort. An emitting apparatus in the shell gives its position, while the shell itself can carry explosives or germs. Its propulsive power is said to be such that it could threaten Paris, Prague, Brussels, or Warsaw."

Z-7 straightened. "You mean that the shell which struck Times Square was radio-directed?"

"Undoubtedly," Operator 5 declared. "But the most important angle, Chief, is this: our operators in Germany have reported to us that the new German gun is in reality capable of a far greater range. As long as it is an immobile piece, as it may well be, there is absolutely no limitation to its range,—or to the range of any other gun designed and operated along the same lines."

OPERATOR 5 rose briskly, stepped to a corbelled window which opened into the office. Through it, he passed a folded paper he removed from his pocket—the apparently trivial letter he had found hidden in the suite formerly occupied by Radi Havara. He directed crisply:

"Please, ask the chemical lab to attempt to develop this for any secret writing that might be on it. I've already made sure that it isn't written in code, and it isn't a stencil-cipher. Iodine vapor or Universal X* may bring out a message."

---

* AUTHOR'S NOTE: The designation "Universal X" is used here for a developer of secret writing perfected during the war by Code and Cipher Compilation sub-section of the Military Intelligence Division, MI-8. It was found by our Intelligence agents at that time that any invisible writing might be developed by a bath of iodine vapor. The vapor clung to and made visible the paper fibers disturbed by the invisible ink regardless of its chemical character. Immediately, the German Intelligence countered by wetting and drying the entire sheet on which any invisible writing had been done, thus disturbing all the fibers and rendering the iodine-vapor developer ineffective. The chemists of MI-8 then made their supreme discovery, designated here "Universal X,"

Operator 5 returned briskly to the typewriter and again typed a message. Again Z-7 scanned it before it was passed to the chief dispatcher. It read tersely:

TO ALL AGENTS OPERATING OUT OF M-11:
A CHECK IS TO BE MADE IMMEDIATELY IN YOUR RESPECTIVE DISTRICTS FOR A PENTHOUSE USED AS HEADQUARTERS BY RADI HAVARA. IF SUSPICIOUS ACTIVITIES ARE NOTED ABOUT ANY PENTHOUSE, REPORT ITS LOCATION AT ONCE BUT DO NOT ATTEMPT TO ENTER. ENTRANCE BY ANY MAN ALONE WILL RESULT IN CERTAIN DEATH.

Z-7's stubby fingers drummed. "You're certain, then, that Radi Havara is guilty of the deaths of our four agents? But why have you directed a search for her in penthouses instead of ordinary apartments?"

As the door of the communications-room closed upon clattering teletype machines, Jimmy Christopher smiled wryly. "There is no reason to believe, Chief, that Radi Havara did not drive the knives into the hearts of those men with her own exquisitely manicured hand. I suggest an investigation of penthouses because of her method of disposing of their bodies."

"I see! Because some sort of a roof location must have been

which was capable of brining out an invisible writing regardless of any means then known of guarding it against direction. The secret is still an invaluable means of combating hostile espionage today."

used for the release of the balloons and a penthouse is the least suspicious and thus the most likely."

Operator 5 nodded quickly. "It is not difficult to deduce, Chief, exactly what happened to the four men who one after another trailed Radi Havara. Their orders were to locate her headquarters, and therefore they did not arrest her on sight. Her suite at the Montblanc was not, I assure you, her headquarters. The men did not trail her there. Her appearing in public was a lure that led them to her secret penthouse and took them to their deaths."

"They located her true headquarters, then—and died there!"

"Died there," Operator 5 affirmed. "On some high and isolated roof. Even now Radi Havara may be hiding there—even now she must have other collapsed balloons and drums of compressed hydrogen hidden, ready to use them as carriers for the disposal of murdered men. The balloons, like those used during the World War, are not large.* But as a means of disposing of dead bodies, they are devilishly effective.

---

* AUTHOR'S NOTE: During the World War, airplanes were at first used to transport spies across the trenches and into enemy territory. The disadvantage of the airplane as a spy-carrier was its betraying noise. Balloons were brought into use to eliminate this hazard. These balloons were on the average about 25 feet in diameter, contained about 300 cubic meters of gas, could carry one person, and had a travel range of from 25 to 40 miles. Later, balloons were also used to drop cages of carrier pigeons behind the lines, and, still later, radio sets to be used for sending military messages by those sympathetic with the opposing army.

"The balloons can be inflated rapidly and liberated without detection. Once in the air, they are at the mercy of the wind and they cannot be traced. Their use can be credited to the scheming brain of Radi Havara, Chief—to that absolutely ruthless daughter of Satan."

"Even though she escaped you, Operator 5—and a man suffers a grave handicap in a situation such as you found yourself in—it's a great advantage to us to know that she is linked directly with the shell that fell into Times Square at midnight."

Operator 5's lips pinched. "I blundered, Chief. I was fool enough to walk into a trap. Radi Havara set it, and I stepped into it blindly. She's the most dangerous adversary I ever faced and—"

"A trap?" Z-7 demanded quickly.

"Just before midnight," Jimmy Christopher said wryly, "she led me to a building on Times Square for, she said, 'a very special and rather unusual reason'. That reason was to kill me."

"What!"

"Exactly. Our four agents were killed, Chief, and their bodies were dropped into the streets as bait—murder-bait. Radi Havara was playing for me as a victim—and she almost got me."

"I don't understand!" Z-7 objected. "I found a notebook containing Radi Havara's Montblanc address, and this other slip." He passed to Z-7 the scrap on which the cryptic message was written. "Both, Chief, were fakes—more bait."

Z-7'S BLACK eyes shone with a puzzled light.

"I suspected at once that they might be, but I took a chance that they were not. Radi Havara might have launched the dead body of J-4 into the air with such haste, I thought, that she would have no time to search his pockets and remove his note-book. I know now that she acted, not with haste, but with devil-ish cunning. She deliberately wrote her Montblanc address into J-4's notebook in the hope that it would lead me there. And for another reason, of which I'm not yet sure, she inserted that cryptic message signed 'V-44' between the leaves."

"She deliberately planned that you should go to the Mont-blanc after her?" Z-7 asked in amazement.

"She did. She dared tell me that she was expecting me—and it was the truth! She must have had one of her agents waiting in the lobby. That person must have telephoned her in her room immediately I appeared. She came down at once to lure me after her. Her only reason for going to the Falker Building was to trick me into being there at midnight—when she knew the shell would fall! Her purpose from the very beginning was to kill me—and into that trap I walked as innocent as you please!"

"Her reason for wanting you out of the way is that she real-ized you are by far her most dangerous adversary!"

Tim Donovan, sitting tensely in a chair at the side of the office, had listened alertly to the conversation. He interjected quickly: "The explosion would've killed us too, Chief, if Jimmy hadn't taken advantage of that safe!"

Operator 5 smiled. "Her one slip-up in an otherwise perfect murder trap, Z-7. The safe was an old one that hadn't been taken from the building because it wasn't worth the cost of moving it. It was impossible to sound a warning when I saw that shell coming, because I knew only a few seconds would pass before it struck. The safe was the only possible shelter. It was, even so, a chance—but I'm still on this case, and I'll get Radi Havara yet!"

Z-7 gestured his puzzlement. "Operator 5, I'm still completely in the dark as to her motive. Why has she turned this attack upon us? What does she hope to accomplish?"

"Her purpose," Operator 5 declared incisively, "is to plunge the United States into war."

"Into war? But why? With what nation?"

"That, Chief, is the great question. But we must learn it—soon. There is an intricate pattern of intrigue behind Radi Havara's espionage operations. Her hope is to plunge us into war in order to achieve some vital advantage to the country for which she is working. She has struck only her first blow. I assure you that more will follow."

Z-7 stared at the perfumed slip bearing the cryptic message. "You base that statement on this?"

"That message, even though it is bait put out for me by Radi Havara, must be heeded. I'm sure that it means much. When that woman speaks the truth—as I'm sure that message does, Chief—it means danger!"

"First time midnight tonight every twelve thereafter" Z-7 quoted. "My God! Does this mean that new attacks will be launched at us at regular intervals?"

"It means exactly that! The attacks upon us have barely begun! The nation which has launched this drive upon us is acting upon the utmost desperation—determined to achieve its secret purpose even at the cost of the destruction of the United States!" Z-7 SAT motionless, his face paled, his black eyes smoldering into those of Operator 5. Silence reigned in the soundproofed office—silence broke at last by the rasp of a buzzer on the desk. Operator 5 shot a quick glance at a flashing bulb on a small annunciator and rose quickly. "The lab is calling, Chief!"

With Z-7 and Tim Donovan following quickly, he strode along a corridor to a room in the rear of the secret suite. Its walls were shelved, loaded with bottled chemical reagents and glittering glass apparatus. Its tables were crowded with beakers, burners, test-tube racks, titrators; there were huge sinks and a black gas-hood. Bending over a desk on which pans of developing solutions sat, a man in an acid-stained smock was examining a dripping sheet of paper—the letter found by Operator 5 in Radi Havara's Montblanc suite.

Gustav Heist, chemist in special service to the Intelligence, turned to Operator 5 with a shrug. "Universal X brings out no message," he declared in his thick accent. "If there is secret writing here, it has been applied in some way that has not affected the fibers of the paper at all."

Operator 5 took the wet sheet carefully. "Let's use the black light." He stepped to another table where a glittering piece of apparatus sat. Above its flat platform, an upright supported a polished reflector in which two carbon candles were poised point to point. Jimmy Christopher threw a switch and brought the points together; immediately a brilliant arc sputtered, and white light coned down.

He snapped out the laboratory globes; he slid a sheet of purple ultra-heat-resisting glass beneath the reflector. Immediately the glare disappeared. Down upon the platform shafted ultra-violet rays invisible to the human eye. Upon it, Operator 5 carefully placed the wet letter.

Immediately a message appeared—words scrawled in flowing script across the page—shining with a ghostly luminescence.

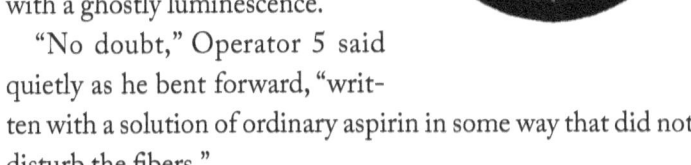

"No doubt," Operator 5 said quietly as he bent forward, "written with a solution of ordinary aspirin in some way that did not disturb the fibers."

Z-7, swiftly reading the hidden message, blurted in appalled amazement: "Good God! It's—" And he broke off. The glowing words read:

> Your wireless reports received. I commend you upon your thorough preparations. Operator 5 must be eliminated at all costs since he alone is shrewd enough to discover our real purpose. Now we are ready to reclaim for the Empire that territory which still belongs rightfully to the Crown—the United States. Its treasures are ours. Our salvation depends upon them—no power now can keep them from us. The United States will soon return to our dominion. God save the King!

Operator 5 straightened, his eyes gleaming darkly. Z-7 stared in a paralysis of bewilderment. "Then *that* is the nation which is attacking us! *That* is the power striving to rule us!"

He peered again at the glowing, scrawled signature affixed to the document. It was the name of the Chief of the Intelligence Service of Great Britain!

CHAPTER 5
THE STROKE OF DOOM

O PERATOR 5 strode briskly along the corridor and into the inner office with the dazed Z-7 and Tim Donovan following. He swung open the door of the communications-room and through the clatter asked the chief dispatcher: "Have we any operators working around Times Square now?"

"Yes."

"Ask the next man who reports to obtain if possible a fragment of the shell. He is to bring it to the laboratory here for a complete chemical analysis."

He closed the door and turned to Z-7. "The Englishman whom I asked to be taken from the Montblanc in an ambulance, Chief—was he brought here?"

Confusedly Z-7 answered: "Yes. We have been holding him so that you might question him. So far he has said nothing. Operator 5 tipped a cam on the Dictaphone on the desk and spoke crisply into the transmitter: "Bring the prisoner into Z-7's office at once!" He took a chair, his eyes clouding thoughtfully, his fingers straying to the death-charm on his watch-chain. Z-7 eyed him intently.

"Great Scott!" the chief blurted breathlessly. "That secret message means that the British Government is behind these attacks! The Mother Country has turned upon us! Europe is an armed camp whose leaders have gone mad!"*

* AUTHOR'S NOTE: The declaration that Europe is an armed camp has been made frequently, but few published statements have gone far toward substantiating it. The following are significant facts. Austria has been frantically arming itself over a long period with the aid of Mussolini, and now provides an open route for arms to Hungary. In Belgium, critics of armament have been silenced, and 600,000,000 Belgian francs are being spent for the building of forts. In Czechoslovakia, the Skoda armament works, the Aussiger-Verein chemical plant and the Brno arms works are operating night and day. England has perfected a new projectile weighing nearly a ton which is able to pierce toughest armor plate equal in thickness to its own caliber and thereafter travel nine miles. The English Admiralty is building 25 battle-cruisers at a cost of $25,000,000 each. England has also perfected the first airplane to fire shells, and is experimenting feverishly with explosives and lethal gas. In Paris, 25,000 gas shelters have been erected. France now has 6,000 airplanes ready for war service. In Germany, all munitions and chemical works are going full blast; in 1934, 1,354,331,500 marks were appropriated for military and semi-military purposes; she is said to have a secret air force far outnumbering that of France. Italy is constructing nine heavy and ten light cruisers; 2,000,000 boys are being given military training. Poland is spending 800,000,000 zloty on military planes. Russia has sent 250,000 picked troops to her Far Eastern frontier. Switzerland is fortifying herself against possible invasion from the north, at a cost of 90,000,000 Swiss francs. Turkey has enlarged her air force and by order of the government, gas cellars are being dug in every city and town. These facts, appalling as they are, can only hint the true conditions within the "armed camp of Europe."

"It is quite true, Chief," Operator 5 said quietly, "that espionage activities all over the world are making it possible for war to strike in any direction at any moment. We know, for instance, that spies have offered to sell to European and Asiatic nations the plans of our new combat planes and of our new 65-mile-an-hour tank. In seven months of this year, the government of France arrested and convicted seventeen spies—among them the Robert Switzes, Americans who were certainly not working for this government. We know that the British government also has recently lost valuable plans to spies.* In the face of such deep

* AUTHOR'S NOTE: Under date of August 3, the International News Service sent the following dispatch from Portsmouth, England:

"Great Britain mobilized her police and her secret service forces today in an effort to solve the mystery of the disappearance of important admiralty documents said to have contained naval secrets of great value to certain foreign powers. The papers, it was reported, concerned tests made of new naval vessels and guns."

The reader will recall, as an example of present-day counter-espionage operations, the case of Norman Baillie-Stewart, 24-year-old subaltern of the Seaforth Highlanders, who was held prisoner in the Tower of London and later convicted of flagrant violations of the Official Secrets Act. The court-martial of Baillie-Stewart was held *in camera* and the significance of his operations will never be disclosed, but the fact that he was discovered reveals that the British Secret Service had without doubt an operator on the

intrigues, Chief, our own foreign espionage system is woefully under-funded."*

Z-7 peered at a huge map of the country spread upon a wall of the office.

"We have considered our position on this continent one of security," he declared, grimly, "believing our neighbors to be permanently friendly. Over three thousand miles of border stretch between the United States and Canada—not one foot of it is fortified! Canada—Dominion of Great Britain—"

"Chief," Operator 5 interrupted thoughtfully, "I have already explained that Radi Havara has devised diabolical pitfalls for us. I admit that the evidence so far points toward Great Britain as our attacker. Yet—"

A KNOCK sounded on the door. Operator 5 strode to open it upon the lean, sharp-faced man whom he had encountered in

---

inside of the German espionage service to which the young officer passed details concerning the latest mechanical devices of the British Army.

There is no question either that a web of the shrewdest espionage and counter-espionage systems is spread over the entire world, particularly over Europe and the United States.

* AUTHOR'S NOTE: No nation officially admits that it employs a spy system, yet it is known that every nation does exactly that. The United States is no exception. The State Department makes use of a secret fund which never appears in the budget and for which no accounting is ever made. It is used by the government to pay for its spies at secret work the world over. The espionage activities of the U.S. government are, however, conducted upon a smaller scale than those of any other world power.

the Montblanc suite of the woman espionage agent. No word was spoken as the tall man entered the room. Though Z-7 gestured him to a chair, he remained rigidly standing. Operator 5 rounded the desk to face him.

"You realize that you are under arrest as an espionage agent?"

"I do."

"Your name?"

"That I will not tell you."

"It does not matter," Operator 5 answered quietly. "We know that you are Agent V-44 of the British Intelligence Service."

The tall man's face turned white.

"We know that you, working hand in hand with Radi Havara, are partly responsible for the attacks made upon New York tonight."

The secret agent's lips pinched hard.

"Perhaps," Operator 5 suggested softly, "yours is a name taken from a compilation similar to the 'Book of the 47,000.'" *

The lean man's eyes flashed with a gleam of terror; but he stood motionless and spoke no word.

---

* AUTHOR'S NOTE: It is a little known fact that before the outbreak of the World War, the German secret service prepared a list, which later became known as the "Book of the 47,000," of women and men, British subjects, known to be guilty of moral lapses or otherwise vulnerable to blackmail. The purpose of the list was to influence those whose names appeared upon it, under threat of exposing scandals, to act as spies for Germany. Thus the "Book of the 47,000" was a weapon of blackmail and bribery to induce men and women to betray their country.

Z-7 stepped forward angrily. He thrust under the prisoner's eyes the scrap of paper that Operator 5 had taken from the notebook of the dead J-4. He demanded: "You wrote this?"

"No!"

"But you *are* V-44! You have worked with Radi Havara! You realize that now you are friendless—that you will be repudiated, as all spies are repudiated when caught, by your native country. You need not look for Radi Havara to lift one lovely finger to help you now!"

"I am not expecting help," the lean man declared grimly. "I—I've been a fool and I—!" He broke off abruptly, his face lined with pain.

Z-7's knuckles rapped the desk. "We admit to you freely," he said in a level tone, "that we are appalled by this revelation. Great Britain is the last nation on the face of the earth we would suspect of launching such a horrible attack upon us. Yet now I realize that the preparations have been going on for months— that your country has turned from economic warfare upon us to armed attack!"

Still the foreign agent stood silent.

"Last summer," Z-7 continued grimly, "your Secretary of the Committee on Imperial Defense, Sir Maurice Hankey, went on a 'secret mission' to all British Dominions. It had to do, for one thing, with the 1935 naval conference. The plans of your government are to augment her fleet from one-third to one-half after 1935. Your country intends, with its aggregate tonnage and its naval bases, to remain undisputed mistress of the seas. Sir Maurice Hankey's message to the Dominions was that, if they expected Great Britain to aid them in any emergency, they must be prepared to stand by the Mother Country.* That was a move of preparation—and now you have acted!"

THE MAN known as V-44 maintained his cold silence. Z-7 stepped closer, his black eyes blazing. "Failing in your economic attack upon us, you have been forced to take more desperate measures to save yourself from financial disaster. That, sir, an intercepted secret communication from your Chief of Intelligence makes clear. You have stopped fighting with the exchange** and you are now using big guns against us!

---

* AUTHOR'S NOTE: Diligent readers of foreign newspaper dispatches will recall that these statements of Z-7 were published as fact.

** AUTHOR'S NOTE: The people of the United States, and even our financial leaders, were not aware that in 1932 the United States became the target of a rigorous economic warfare. The weapon was that of money exchange. The purpose was to annul our tariff laws, to stimulate the sale of foreign goods in American markets while at the same time hindering the sale of American goods in foreign markets, and to propagate a motive for a cancellation of war debts as the price of economic peace. There is not space here fully to explain the intricate operations of this financial attack which came at us from Japan in the West and Great Britain in the East. It was an open, not a concealed attack, but through its complex technical nature it achieved a kind of secrecy. Briefly, the British Treasury brought into operation at that time an Exchange Equalization Account, so-called, of $750,000,000, for the purpose of debasing the British pound. While prices in England remained stationary, the value of the pound fell on foreign exchanges. This operated to give Great Britain a telling advantage in trade with the United States. Under

"The very fact that your government has enlisted the services of Radi Havara," Z-7 shot at the silent man, "means that it is desperately in earnest in this attempt to subjugate us!"

Operator 5 gazed intently at the silent espionage agent. He reached to touch a cam on the Dictaphone. The door of the communications-room snapped open; a clattering surge from the teletype instruments invaded the office; the chief dispatcher strode briskly to the desk.

"We have discovered information," Jimmy Christopher told him quietly while the man known as V-44 listened, "that a secret wireless station is operating somewhere in or near New York, sending messages to a foreign government. It is probably a small short-wave transmitter and it probably operates at

the control of British government financiers, the pound fell by one-third of its value, as low as $3.14. It is also not generally known that, by abandoning the gold standard, in April, 1933, the United States launched a heavy counter-attack in this economic war. The effect of debasing the dollar was to raise the value of the pound in comparison, thereby eliminating England's trade advantage. In spite of the fact that Great Britain immediately weighted her exchange operations with a still greater Equalization Fund, the United States countered to maintain the comparative exchange level and even to strike a balance more favorable to itself than had existed under normal conditions. These funds are still operating. At this writing the British pound is quoted not at its normal figure of $4.86, but at $5.10, and the advantage is with the United States, It should be made clear that the power behind this economic attack was not the Bank of England, but the British Treasury—the government of Great Britain.

irregular periods. You are to begin using at once all your available equipment for the location of this station. Once you spot it, you are to intercept all messages it might send out. These orders are important."

"Yes, sir!"

Jimmy Christopher stepped quietly out of the office, signaled Tim Donovan after him. He shut the adjoining room tightly; he spoke quietly to the boy. "Tim, I have a job for you—an extremely important, dangerous job. You got a good look at that man in there, old-timer. I want you to slip out of here, wait in the street, keeping a taxi handy. If you see that man come out later, I want you to follow him. Even if he is with several of our agents, Tim, stick close. No matter what happens, keep him in sight."

THE BOY eagerly slipped out a cork-lined door, flashing a broad grin at Operator 5. Jimmy Christopher quietly reentered Z-7's office. The Washington Chief was still questioning the foreign espionage agent vehemently; his only answer was silence. He rapped his knuckles on the desk in his exasperation.

"Chief, we're wasting time," Operator 5 said quickly. "The crew of that disguised airplane carrier destroyed themselves rather than risk being seized and forced to betray the nation they were serving. This man is operating in the same system. He will not talk. Therefore I suggest that we transfer him at once to Address K. There, I think, he will change his mind.

"Address K," Operator 5 continued quietly, "is a house especially equipped to encourage talkativeness in men of your taciturn temperament I regret the necessity of send you there; I'm sure you'll regret it even more, but you leave us no alternative."

V-44's eyes glinted with fear he could not control. He jerked nervously as the door of the office opened with a snap and two men entered. At the Chief's gesture, they stationed themselves beside V-44.

"You're to take this man to Address K at once," he directed them. "Keep a close watch upon him. While you are on your way, I will telephone the keeper of Address K exactly what measures are to be used upon him. Report back at once."

Z-7's gesture signaled the agents out. Operator 5 bent quickly over the desk, scribbled on a slip of paper as the pair seized V-44 and turned him away. One of the Intelligence agents bound a handkerchief tightly about the lean man's eyes; they moved toward the door. When they had passed through, and as the door was about to close, Jimmy Christopher slipped the square of paper into the hand of the second man out.

Z-7 peered curiously at Operator 5. "What the devil!" he exclaimed. "You led that spy to believe we intend to torture his information out of him. We never do anything of the sort. We have no such place as Address K. We've carried your subterfuge through—but why?"

"My object," Operator 5 declared grimly, "is to break through the web of deception that Radi Havara has spun. It's to find information that we can trust. So far, Chief, we have made scant headway. One attempt after another has been made to trap us. We're fighting the most devilish system of espionage that ever operated. As to what this move will achieve—we can only wait!"

Operator 5's darkened eyes turned to the closed door. Beyond it a man was standing—the Intelligence agent to whom he had

No car was moving over the rutted snow

save the taxi carrying Tim Donovan.

V-44 raced straight toward it!

passed the hastily-written message. S-3 was his designation; he was one of the most trusted men working out of M-11. He peered now upon scrawled words which carried an astounding order:

Allow the prisoner to escape.

THE MURK of a drab dawn filled the snow-drifted street. Quiet pervaded the neighborhood of exclusive shops. Beside the windows of Marielle's salon, a door opened quietly, and an Intelligence operator stepped from it He glanced warily back and forth; but alert as he was he did not detect the fact that a boy was watching from a dark doorway far toward the next corner. Tim Donovan was on the job.

A sedan—one of a fleet of cars at the disposal of the Intelligence Service—spun around the corner from Fifth Avenue. As it drew to a stop, the Intelligence agent waiting at the curb signaled. From the doorway the other operator stepped quickly, guiding a third man who was blindfolded—V-44. They entered the car quickly; the door, its curtains drawn, clacked shut. Tim Donovan watched.

Inside the car, S-3 passed to his fellow agent the scribbled order of Operator 5. C-6 read it in silent amazement. Quickly S-3 turned and thrust the slip toward the uniformed operator acting as chauffeur. He stared at it, nodded shortly, and threw the car into gear. Immediately, as it whirred off, S-3 jerked down a blind that covered the fore-window, and snapped on a dome-light.

Tim Donovan jumped down snow-covered steps as the sedan whirred past. He walked rapidly around the corner, to the taxi which he had ordered to wait. He climbed in, pointed to the turning sedan, and perched alertly on the seat to watch. The cab lurched from the curb, travelling southward after the sedan.

The man at the wheel of the taxi growled: "That driver's drunk!" Across the avenues, deeper into the East Side, the sedan scurried crazily. It weaved from curb to curb; its wheels spun and caught and spun again. Tim Donovan, puzzled, snapped orders at his reluctant driver in his determined effort to keep it in sight. Then again it swung to turn southward—swung so sharply that it spun half around on the snow and then, with a sudden spurt drove hard across the curb and full against an iron post.

The resounding crash echoed up and down the deserted street. The sedan's bumper buckled and the post bit deep into the radiator. Steam sizzled and the headlamps blinked out as the cramped wheels whirled the sedan in its rebound! It slithered against the curb and wrenched over. A second rasping crash sounded—and the car lay on its side in snow.

Tim Donovan started from his seat as he saw the car lurch over. While its wheels spun, the door on its upper side was flung open. Through the body sprang the tall man, known only as V-44. As he twisted to slam the door down behind him, S-3's head and shoulders appeared. The Intelligence operator groped wildly for the foreign spy.

V-44 struck viciously. The blow caught S-3 on the side of the head as the U.S. agent jerked up his automatic. V-44 followed with a second savage blow, snatched at the weapon. S-3 lurched backward; the door whacked down above him. The foreign agent whirled into a crazy run along the street.

NO PEDESTRIANS were near. No car was moving over the rutted snow save the taxi carrying Tim Donovan. V-44 raced straight toward the cab!

Tim Donovan saw him sprinting close, saw him gesturing frantically for the taxi to stop. "Go ahead!" the boy gasped but V-44 flung himself directly into the car's way. The driver twisted the wheel sharply to avoid striking the desperate man. The taxi skidded crazily. It struck the curb, spun again to face the storefronts.

"Stop! Wait!" V-44's call sounded sharply. Tim Donovan slid from the seat and ducked below the windows. The cab-driver threw into reverse gear, and the rear wheels of the taxi rasped. V-44, circling, reached through the open window to grip the driver's collar. "Get out! Get out, or by God—!"

A violent jerk dragged the driver half through the window. He snapped the door-catch and sprawled out. As he swayed up, V-44 swung the automatic desperately. A sharp crack sounded is it struck the driver's head. He went down.

V-44 slipped behind the wheel with anxious haste. He slammed the taxi forward, jounced it over the curb. He twisted it into the street, glancing wildly back at the overturned Intelligence sedan. Its door was still closed; the two U.S. agents had not appeared. V-44 jammed the accelerator down.

The cab whined swiftly southward along the avenue while Tim Donovan crouched out of sight—an escaping spy chauffeuring him!

The taxi, almost thirty minutes later, slithered to the curb as the man at the wheel swerved it recklessly. The door clacked open. Tim Donovan heard crunching footfalls in the snow, raised himself to see V-44 hurrying toward a gloomy doorway set in a blank brick wall. He slipped hastily out the opposite door, huddled behind the car to watch.

Tim Donovan had lived all his life in New York; in his boot-blacking days he had wandered over every street in lower Manhattan. He found himself now close to City Hall Park and Park Row. Beyond rose the span of the Brooklyn Bridge, rumbling with subway cars and increasing traffic. To a rear entrance of an old building within the shadow of the bridge, V-44 had hurried.

The bleak door swung open upon darkness; the secret agent passed through and immediately it began to close. Tim Donovan darted forward. Alertly he jerked his handkerchief from his pocket. At the instant when the narrowing crack of the door almost disappeared, he thrust the handkerchief into it. Immediately he whirled away, turned his back to the door, and walked.

A MOMENT he paused there, then he crossed the narrow street and observed, as he passed, the handkerchief still lodged in the crack. He hurried to the door. Carefully he pushed at the knob; and his breath caught when it responded. His handkerchief had accomplished his hoped-for purpose; it had prevented the spring bolt on the inside of the door from catching in its socket. Swiftly he stepped through, backing to the door, closing it behind him.

He looked into utter darkness; he was enveloped by dank air. He felt his way forward to the top of a flight of steps he could not see. He hesitated, remembering that Operator 5 had urged him to report, but he could not be sure that this was V-44's destination. The spy might, he knew, be seeking a way through a basement, intending to leave again by an entrance on another street, or planning to slip into the subway. The possibility that halting the chase now might cost him his quarry urged Tim Donovan forward into the musty darkness. He felt his way downward into a growing silence. The rumble of the city faded away. The flight of steps was of brick, and amazingly long. It angled deep beneath the street level; its air carried a quiet warmth and a rich odor of oldness. Tim Donovan judged that he was at least forty feet below the street when he reached a stone platform on which a dim light shone.

Farther down, at the base of another mossy flight, stood an archway beyond which rose crusted brick walls. Above the arch figures in peeling paint read: *1868*. From some far point beyond came a rustle of movement, a faint echo of steps.

Tim Donovan crept down to the archway, peered through into damp, spacious rooms filled with stacked wooden cases. Their inscriptions were in European languages; they contained, Tim realized, stores of wine. The stony crypt was far beneath streets which teemed daily with thousands who knew nothing of it.

Tim Donovan eased into the silent room, and saw that it was one of a series extending far on both sides, each of which was filled with cases of imported wine. Globes burning in wrought-iron fixtures filled them with a dim yellow glow. Tim Donovan drifted on. Searching for another way out, he saw none.

He came into a room in which old furniture sat around an ancient table; in its end wall stood a door, closed. Sheets of papers lay on the table; they were evidently an incompleted inventory. A telephone sat near them. Tim Donovan's eyes brightened and he darted to it, brought the receiver to his ear.

Suddenly, without warning, the closed door flashed open. In a shaft of brighter light a lean figure appeared: V-44. He became a motionless silhouette when he glimpsed Tim Donovan. The boy, eyes widened, frantically rattled the telephone hook as he backed away. With a sudden snarl, the lean man leaped, and into his hand glinted the automatic he had snatched from S-3.

He struck viciously as the boy dropped the instrument and sprang away. His powerful hand gripped Tim Donovan's arm. Tim spun frantically, driving out his hard fists, as the gun-butt slashed toward him. He jerked his head aside, and the blow glanced downward against his cheek, but its power was enough to stun him. He staggered blindly as the lean man banded him with strong arms.

HIS WRISTS were twisted behind him; a rope was lashed around them while the blood throbbed through his fingers. His kicking feet were looped together tightly. He rugged desperately and hopelessly at his bonds as he was dragged up and thrust against the cold wall. The big automatic in the hand of V-44 hit hard against his chest.

"Quiet!" Again the foreign agent whipped rope around him. Tim Donovan was bound to an ancient oaken upright less when V-44 stepped back. The spy's lean face was hardened cruelly; his eyes glittered with rage.

"You followed me! You were trying to telephone Operator 5! You'll never live to do that now!"

Tim Donovan glared his defiance as the blurted words echoed into the hollowness of the damp room. V-44 turned away quickly, stepped through the door, closed it. Tim Donovan heard his voice rumble as he spoke over the telephone. Dazedly the boy stared around him, his eyes brimming with tears of fury.

The bright gleam of overhead bulbs glittered over apparatus sitting upon a table close to Tim Donovan. He recognized it as a short-wave receiver-transmitter. On the near corner the key was affixed. The boy's eyes widened at it.

If he could reach the switch and that key! Jimmy Christopher had taught Tim Donovan the Morse code. A year ago they had dot-dashed messages to each other, from one room to another of the home of Operator 5's father, until the boy had attained skin and speed in sending and receiving messages. The wireless set, once in operation, would sputter its signals into the ether—and the experts at M-11 were trying even then to search out that station. The chances were thousands to one that the signals might never be heard. Yet, if Tim Donovan could reach that key—if he could free one hand and throw the switch and reach that key....

Desperately, while the voice of V-44 carried from the adjoining room, he tried to wrest his right hand from the snug loop of rope that imprisoned it. While his blood pounded hot, while his skin rubbed raw, while he clenched his jaw against the pain that throbbed through him—he tried....

CHAPTER 6
SCHEDULED DOOM

THE DOOR of the communications-room of Intelligence Headquarters M-11 snapped open. The chief dispatcher reported quickly: "S-3 reports his prisoner escaped in a taxi—headed south!"

"Have him report back to M-11!" Operator 5 snapped. He

glanced up at the chief dispatcher. "You're trying to locate that wild-cat wireless station?"

"Yes, sir! There are a number of transmitters operating now, but they're all accounted for and none is sending code."

Operator 5 spoke crisply again to the waiting chief-dispatcher. "Stick to that job. And when any report comes from Tim Donovan by telephone, shoot it through to me at once."

While Z-7 was speaking quietly over the telephone, a dispatcher entered quickly, carrying a teletype message. When the Washington chief finished he turned to read it:

... M-11... DISGUISED AIRPLANE CARRIER WAS THE KITCHENER... OWNED BY BRITISH SHIPPING FIRM OF CRUTHERS LTD... OPERATING OUT OF LIVERPOOL... DETAILS FOLLOW.... T-3....

Z-7's fist banged the desk. "Every bit of evidence we find points toward Great Britain as our attacker!"

Jimmy Christopher toyed thoughtfully with the golden death-charm dangling from his watch-chain. "It is evidence, Chief," he said quietly, "which cannot be trusted."

"Not trusted? When, without exception—"

Z-7 broke off, lifted from the desk a report which had been received at M-11 earlier that morning:

... M-11... ENEMY BOMBERS DROPPED INTO BAY CARRY NO IDENTIFYING MARKS BUT ARE WITHOUT DOUBT OF BRITISH MANUFACTURE... E-9....

OPERATOR 5 leaned close. "True, Chief that these reports

prove the airplane carrier and the radio planes originated in England, but they do not prove that Great Britain has used them against us. It is possible that they were acquired by another European power."

"And the letter you discovered in Radi Havara's rooms? The letter signed by the Chief of the British Intelligence Service?"

"Forged," Jimmy Christopher declared. "More bait, Chief. A trick of Radi Havara's."

"You mean that some other European power has gone to these great lengths to make it appear that Great Britain is the aggressor against us when in reality she is not?"

"I mean exactly that Radi Havara left the message in her rooms with the intention that I should find it—that we should believe England guilty! The message signed by V-44 is another similar trick. V-44 denied writing it, and I'm inclined to believe him. We dare not lose sight, Chief, of the only possible reason there can be for the activities of that woman spy now."

"To plunge the United States into war in order to gain an advantage with the country she is secretly serving!"

"To plunge us into war," Operator 5 agreed quietly, "with Great Britain!"

Again the door of the communications-room opened, and a dispatcher strode in. He placed a scrawled sheet in front of Operator 5 and explained tersely: "Operator F-8, stationed at Police Headquarters, just telephoned that a taxi-driver has reported his cab stolen from him by an armed man whose description checks with that of our prisoner, V-44. The driver says he had a boy as passenger but does not know what became of him."

Jimmy Christopher eyed the report gravely as the dispatcher left. Z-7 read the scrawl and blurted: "Tim was in that cab! My God! V-44 was desperate when he made that 'escape'—he would not stop at murder to get away!"

Again Operator 5's fingers strayed to his death-charm. "I sent Tim on a dangerous job, Chief. If it's humanly possible for him to do so—if nothing serious has happened to him—he'll report. We can only wait."

Z-7 drummed nervously. Jimmy Christopher leaned forward, his voice sharpened: "Chief, there are excellent reasons—less tangible than this evidence, I admit—to believe that Great Britain is not guilty of the attacks made upon us. First of all, though England did engage in an economic war against us, Japan took part in it even more ruthlessly, and since the yen is greatly debased, is still doing so. England is being damaged by the Japanese financial guns even now. It is logical to suppose she might attempt to eliminate Japan's greater economic advantage, but not our lesser one.

"And again, you have only to remember the financial burden of the last war in order to realize that for England to start another war would not aid her a penny's worth economically. It would, instead, be economic suicide—for the United States as well, if we took part in it." *

* Author's Note: It may surprise the reader to learn that France, even while in imminent danger of being utterly crushed by the German invasion during

"TRUE!" Z-7 admitted. "Another war would bankrupt the world. No country can support a new burden of war while the weight of the last is still resting upon us. Yet the great armament manufacturers are exerting their power now—merciless organizations which provoke war in order to sell their materials. They, together with the operations of present-day espionage rings, are so strong that—"

"We must look elsewhere for the real power behind the attack upon us, Chief," Operator 5 broke in. "England, I assure you, is not that power. Italy could not be. Russia is far too occupied with the Siberian-Japanese crisis. Austria is full of internal turmoil. France dare not turn as aggressor upon us while she is threatened by Germany. Germany has her hands still full of the recent

the World War, obliged the British and United States governments to pay dearly for the privilege of saving her. France collected from both allies vast sums for the use of trenches in which Tommies and Yanks fought shoulder-to-shonlder with exhausted *poilus*. Britain and the United States paid France also for the use of ports and bases, and France collected duties on materials sent to her by England and the United States for the construction of piers necessary for the landing of the expeditionary forces. France welcomed the troops with hysterical joy while keeping strict accounts against them and obliging them to pay even for the water they drank. The United States paid these costs in gold, while France borrowed from this government vast sums which constitute the war debts that she has since repudiated.

threatened revolt, and Hitler will not act until the power behind his speaks the word.*

"Therefore, Chief, we must look elsewhere. There are no other possibilities save the smaller states of Europe. The new European war will crush down upon them. In this great conflict, they face the threat of utter destruction, and they will be almost

---

* AUTHOR'S NOTE: The significance of Operator 5's statement concerning Germany and Hitler may be briefly explained. The facts are little known.

On July 30, Hitler crushed an imminent revolt by the Storm Troops. For ten days prior to that date, the General Staff of the Army, though they do not usually do so, carried their service revolvers. They had learned that the Storm Troops planned to massacre them and seize control of the Army. The master-mind behind this plot was Ernst Roehm, commander of the Storm Troops. If it had succeeded it would have gone down in history as one of the world's most extraordinary revolts. Hitler, learning of the conspiracy, staged his bloody "putsch" and crushed it, thus avoiding a terrific civil war. At this writing, the aftermath of this event is still of great concern to the Reichsführer.

Fritz Thyssen, head of the Vereinigte Stahlwerke, the German Steel trust, is the man who brought Hitler into power, and who keeps him there. The government of France believes that Germany is rearming with the direction and support of Thyssen. Thyssen has behind him a tremendous weight of industrial and financial power. Students of the European situation believe that Hitler will endure only as long as Thyssen wishes; that Thyssen is preponderantly the man whose power is sufficient to plunge all of Europe into a new war whenever he chooses that war to break out.

helpless to save themselves.* Most dangerous of those states is one possessing a strength out of all proportion to its size. Its men are patriots to the death, no country on earth burns with a greater desire to perpetuate itself. 'The Bulldog of Europe,' Chief—Urakia!"

"I can well believe," Z-7 declared grimly, "that Urakia is capable of taking any desperate measure to save itself from the threat of extinction in the next war, but so far,—"

"So far," Operator 5 declared, "we have not a particle of evidence to prove Urakia is behind the attack. If it is, Chief, her motive is plain—only too plain. By plunging the United States into war with Great Britain, or with any other nation in Europe,

---

* AUTHOR'S NOTE: To this statement of Operator 5's, the following cable dispatch from Belgrade, published recently, is pertinent:

"The Serbs, Austrians and Hungarians who began the last war twenty years ago are resigned, twenty years later, to the inevitability of the next. As small states, they see a situation beyond their own control, and they do not trust the statesmanship of the great powers.

"The balance of power is shifting dangerously in the area of certain countries in Central Europe, where so many of Europe's wars in the past were fought.

"The Great Powers have not yet built a League of Nations to which a small state can go without allies and champions to demand justice and equality of treatment."

This dispatch means, briefly, that without war allies, the small Central European nations face extinction; yet if, in choosing an ally, they go to war with a power which suffers defeat, they again face certain destruction. The situation is one which has aroused the governments of these countries to desperation.

it will thereby shift the battle area far away from its own borders. The desperate strategy of a nation frantically striving to save itself from being wiped off the map of the world!"

Z-7 jerked up. "The government and the people of Urakia are precisely of that temperament! They would not hesitate to scheme to throw two great world powers into a devastating war in, order to preserve themselves!"

"Depend upon it, Chief," Operator 5 declared emphatically, "that is exactly the motive behind Radi Havara's operations. Whether she is working for Urakia or some other Central European nation, she has set a trap that may betray the United States into destroying itself."

A KNOCK sounded on the door. In answer to Z-7's call it opened to admit a mild mannered secret agent, T-9. He advanced to the desk briskly and reported:

"I have just come from duty at Times Square, Chief. Following Operator 5's orders, I found a fragment of the shell, and I've already taken it into the lab for analysis. Heist promises a report within a few hours."

"Good!" Operator 5 rose. "That's all, T-9." He stepped toward the door of the communications-room. He trust it open, demanded of the chief-dispatcher: "That report come?"

"Not yet!"

Jimmy Christopher returned to his desk, his eyes darkened with anxiety. He strode across the room and back, glanced haggardly at the electric clock on Z-7's desk.

"There's still nothing we can do, Chief, but wait for reports.

Tim is following our most important lead. He'll come through—I know he'll come through."

Jimmy Christopher broke off, taking up from the desk the perfumed slip which carried the cryptic message signed with the designation, V-44. His lips formed the words: "Every twelve thereafter," and his dark gaze turned to the clock. Time had passed slowly, yet with appalling rapidity. The hands of the time-piece, as Operator 5 waited, swung toward noon.

When the communications-door opened he sprang to his feet. The chief-dispatcher hurried forward with a yellow report.

"From Tim?"

"No—no word yet from him."

Operator 5 took the yellow sheets slowly. "Not heard? Then—"

He broke off abruptly and again paced back and forth across the office. His gaze turned repeatedly to the electric clock on Z-7's desk. Minute by minute the hour of twelve o'clock drew nearer. As the minute hand approached the mark, Jimmy Christopher stood motionless, eyes darkened, nerves tight.

High noon passed.

He resumed his pacing. He read reports that were brought from the communications-room, but none of them was from Tim Donovan. None of them reported progress on the case at hand. Operator 5 sat at his desk, lost in thought. He did not stir until the hands of the clock had marked the passage of almost an hour.

"Almost noon," he said quietly to himself, "in the Central Standard Time belt. Almost—"

HE JERKED up as the door snapped open and a dispatcher

entered thrusting a yellow sheet toward him. Operator 5's shoulders sagged when he saw that it was not from Tim Donovan. It read:

> … M-11 NY… UNABLE TO FIND ANY EVIDENCE INDICATING THAT A CANNON OF UNUSUALLY LONG RANGE WAS MADE IN ANY STEEL PLANT IN THIS COUNTRY… PHP.…

From the communications-room, a third dispatcher hurried excitedly. He flashed a flimsy toward Operator 5. Breathlessly he blurted: "I've been trying to pick up that wildcat station. I just spotted it! The message didn't come in code. It—it's from—!"

Jimmy Christopher's gesture silenced that man. His glittering eyes read scrawled words that set his heart to hammering. Over Operator 5's shoulder, Z-7 read:

> 5—5—5—5—Doorway behind Star Building—held prisoner—Tim—

Operator 5 strode to the door. Z-7 jerked after him. Jimmy Christopher's hand whitened on the knob as he snapped the way open. He was hastening through when a sharp call came—a call that stopped him short and caused his face to flash pale as death.

"Another shell!" Operator 5 and Z-7 stared at the frantic, shirt-sleeved man who had hurried from the communications-room. His lips worked soundlessly upon words that would not come. Jimmy Christopher thrust past him toward a glass-walled booth in which a teletype receiver was clattering. With the appalled Z-7 bending beside him, he stared at the yellow strip snaking from the machine:

> … M-11 NY… TERRIFIC EXPLOSION HAS JUST OCCURRED MICHIGAN BOULEVARD… ENTIRE CITY SHAKEN… NO DETAILS POSSIBLE AS YET… INDICATIONS POINT CONCLUSIVELY THAT CONCUSSION WAS BURSTING OF HIGH EXPLOSIVE SHELL… PARTICULARS FOLLOW….

Jimmy Christopher straightened grimly, peering at the huge electric clock on the wall. " 'Every twelve thereafter!' It means—every twelve *hours!*"

Z-7's face was an ashen mask. "Good God! The shell struck in the very heart of Chicago! Nine hundred air miles from the first in Times Square! That damnable gigantic gun—!" He broke off, gazing into Operator 5's night-dark eyes.

"Every twelve hours, Chief! They hit every noon and midnight I Those shells will keep coming—destroying, lolling—until the United States is plunged hopelessly into war—unless we can locate and wreck that big gun first!"

ONLY A few minutes earlier, the great city of Chicago had been following the busy routine of an ordinary business day. The stroke of twelve o'clock had brought chaos bursting down upon it.

A prolonged, rising wail had signaled the coming of disaster. Out of a clear blue sky, the metallic cry swelled, growing in volume, heightening in pitch, chilling the hearts of all who heard. Thousands hurrying along famous Michigan Boulevard paused to peer with terror into the sky. Countless automobiles and cabs stopped with squealing brakes while their passengers scrambled out to stare heavenward. Throughout all the city, the shrill sound rang—the voice of doom!

Across the sky, then, the flash appeared—a streak of white light trailing from the zenith so dazzling bright that it was plainly visible in the glare of the noonday sun. Second by second, the brilliant line lengthened down toward the city while the banshee shriek rose to an ear-drilling intensity. Madly the thousands in the streets began scattering in search of any possible shelter. Like a tidal wave, pandemonium flooded through the city.

All who heard that unearthly shriek, all who saw that comet of doom streaking out of the heavens, knew that the same sign had preluded the horrible disaster that had struck New York—that now, instant by fleeting instant, the same screaming destruction was descending.

High noon—and *explosion!*

Down upon the wide boulevard the shell plunged. The terrific concussion struck across the rearing fronts of great buildings, splintering every window instantly, ripping down masses of masonry that plunged to sidewalks strewn with dead, teeming with the crazed noon-day crowds that had survived the blast. High into the sky and far along the thoroughfare surged thick clouds of fumes, sweeping like a shroud over the fallen. Far into the air flung the power of the explosion, spattering debris over an area of turmoil.

Out of the sky, sounding its warning only by seconds, doom had dropped.

Terror at twelve!

CHAPTER 7
WAR-CLOUDS GATHER

PAST CITY HALL PARK, Operator 5 swung the black, stream-lined roadster—a duplicate of the one which had been destroyed in the Times Square disaster. Z-7, sitting tensely beside him, twisted to listen to the screeching of newsboys running along the sidewalks. Extra editions were pouring from the thundering presses of the city, square black type across the front of them:

> Chicago Struck by Shell at Noon!
> England Believed Attacking U.S.!
> Terror Sweeps Country in New Attack!
> Secret Documents Betray England's Guilt!

The Washington Chief peered haggardly at Operator 5 as the car swung eastward. "How have the newspapers learned that our evidence points to England?"

Jimmy Christopher answered tightly: "More of Radi Havara's work! Somehow she must have passed to the news services more faked evidence to involve Great Britain. That, for her, is an easy trick. She has laid her plans well, Chief!"

The cries of the newsboys followed the car stridently:

Twelve Hours Separates Blasts!
Another Shell May Fall at Midnight!
Next Target of Hidden Big Gun Unknown!
No Spot in Country Safe From Attack!

Operator 5 declared grimly: "That's more of her devilish work! She allowed us to know, through that fake message signed V-44, that the shells will come at twelve hour intervals—and now she has let it leak out to the people. She is deliberately starting a wave of terror in the United States. She is taking every possible opportunity to trick us into war!"

Operator 5's lips pinched tight as he swung the car to the curb. He had scanned the narrow street alertly; he had driven far eastward. Now, slipping from the roadster with Z-7 at his side, he turned back. Behind him lay the East River; above rose the black span of the Brooklyn Bridge; ahead sat City Hall. Jimmy Christopher worked his way through the noonday crowds until he reached a bleak wall broken only by a single drab doorway.

He glanced around sharply, and stepped close. He twisted the knob to find the way locked. His movements casual, he brought from his pocket a leather case of master-keys.*

"My boy," Z-7 said quietly, "I urge you again to call other operators here to help us. We're taking a dangerous chance—"

"A chance that Tim took alone, Chief," Jimmy Christopher

---

* AUTHOR'S NOTE: These master-keys were designed and made by Operator 5 in the workshop of the house in New York designated Address Y, and they are capable of opening any known type of lock.

answered quietly. "I'm thinking most of all of him. If anything has happened to him—"

OPERATOR 5'S words faded away anxiously as he inserted a flat key in the lock. He withdrew it, his eyes narrowed, his lips pressed hard. He tried a second. Z-7, watching him, sensed his deep concern.

A soft click sounded. The third master-key had turned. Operator 5's hand slipped gently toward his arm-pitted holster; he twisted the knob.

Quickly, alertly, he stepped through. Z-7 sidled after him. The door shut to enclose them in dank darkness. They paused, listening into silence, fingers touching the butts of their guns.

Slowly, Operator 5 slid to the top of the brick flight. Soundless steps carried him downward. Heavy quiet surrounded the two silent figures moving with the utmost caution. The flight angled; a faint gleam of light appeared, shafting across a lower platform. Toward it Operator 5 and Z-7 moved; abruptly they stopped, nerves snapped tight, listening.

From above, a click sounded. The noise of the street surged into the musty darkness and faded away again. Gritting noises followed.

Operator 5 leaned close to Z-7, whispered: "Somebody has come in!"

In the yellow silence of the crypt they paused. Plainly then they heard footfalls coming down the brick steps. The cavern echoed the gritting noise. Jimmy Christopher and Z-7 turned rapidly toward the room in whose far wall a closed door stood. The person who had entered was approaching the archway when they whirled behind a stack of wine-cases and huddled against the wall.

Heels thumped into the crypt. A man strode toward the closed door. Immediately it opened and brighter light shafted out. A guttural voice burst:

"You—here! You fool!"

From the doorway, the voice of the man known as V-44 spoke: "Bord! I've been waiting for you! For God's sake, they had me—I had to come here!"

The footfalls passed into the next room. Through the open door, the voice of the man Bord sounded: "That boy! What's he doing here?"

"I thought I'd gotten away clean! I didn't know I was being followed—but he traced me here somehow! He's the only one who knows! Otherwise we're safe, I tell you!"

"Safe? When you've led Operator 5's best friend to this place? You're mad!"

"I tell you, no one else knows!"

"No one else? You're sure! Ah, so! It will be easy enough to fix him so he won't talk! He will never tell that—"

"Bord!" V-44 interrupted sharply. "I came here because I've got to have help to get out of the country! God knows where I'll go, but—"

"Help?" Bord retorted. "You can expect no help from us! You are of no further value to us!" The chesty voice dropped. "Perhaps you were fool enough to tell the United States Intelligence that you are not working for Great Britain but for Urakia—*did you?*"

IN THE darkness behind the stack of crates in the dim room,

Z-7 jerked. He turned widened eyes to see Operator 5 rising grimly.

"No—I told them nothing!" V-44 protested. "God—do you think I'm that much of a weakling? To tell them that I have betrayed my own country? Fool enough to yield to Radi Havara, perhaps, but not—"

A burst of mirthless laughter interrupted. "You come here seeking help! You're mad! Don't you realize that you were brought into our plan only so that you might be captured by the United States Intelligence? Don't you know that your part was only to make them believe Great Britain is involved? You have served our purpose now!"

A stricken silence followed, broken at last by V-44's gasp: "Then that's why Radi Havara called me to the Montblanc! She knew Operator 5 would be there! She deliberately planned that he would capture me and think—"

"Precisely!" Bord broke in heavily. "You, my sorry one, I do not envy. Your chief knows now, certainly, that you have betrayed your service—for a woman! You have made yourself a man without a country! And now you come here seeking help!" Another burst of cruel laughter followed.

V-44's answer was a moan: "Oh, God!"

"Aside, now!" Bord commanded. "I have come here to receive a message. It is time. You—do you think now that you will ever leave this place alive? Your life—it is worth nothing now—nothing, except perhaps so small a thing as a bullet!"

Behind the stack of cases, Operator 5 moved quietly. He sidled into the open and faced the open door. Through it, he saw a corner of the room—the corner in which the wan-faced Tim Donovan was bound to an oaken upright. His lids lowered slowly as he stepped forward without a sound with Z-7 following.

A table was visible also to Jimmy Christopher, and the wireless equipment on it. The two men were out of sight but a shadow fell across the doorway. It was the silhouette of a hand gripping a leveled automatic, the finger curled snugly around the trigger.

V-44's voice sounded breathlessly. "God—what're you going to do?"

"Kill you, my sorry one. Kill you here and now. Then, of course, the boy.... Stop!"

A flicker of black across the doorway was the quick movement of a hand snatching at the automatic. The gun whipped down from the clutching fingers. Instantly the blast of a shot rocked through the hollowness of the crypt. A muffled cry sounded; and a man staggered back, into Operator 5's view.

V-44 retreated with hands clawing at his chest—hands that dripped red. The betrayed British agent sucked in an agonized breath and doubled. He rolled to the floor, sprawled outwardly lay still.

Jimmy Christopher sprang to the doorway. Within the bright room, the thick-trunked man named Bord was whirling upon Tim Donovan. His gun thrust close to the Irish lad's chest. The boy's quick response was a gesture of desperation. He struck out with one free hand—a hand rawed by the excruciating effort that had drawn it from the rope-loops—and grabbed at the gun.

Bord sprang back instantly, snatching the weapon from Tim's numb fingers. "What! You're loose! Then—"

A SMASHING report broke into the blurted words. Operator 5's automatic blazed leaden defiance through the doorway. The bullet spattered on the barrel of Bord's automatic. It spun the ape-like man half around the instant his finger squeezed the trigger. It cracked to the wall beside Tim Donovan. Bord whirled as Operator 5 sprang inward, as the Irish lad twisted in the ropes.

Bord's weapon spat three times, swiftly, as Jimmy Christopher leaped along the inner wall. The bullets spattered on the bricks behind him. His automatic lightninged an answer to the attack. Leaping wildly, Bord flung himself against the far wall. He flung an arm upward, struck an iron lever projecting through the bricks. That arm dropped instantly-pierced by a slug from Jimmy Christopher's gun.

Operator 5 leaped, wrested the gun from Bord, heard the espionage agent utter a bursting, evil laugh, and backed away in amazement.

"Jimmy! Up there!"

Tim Donovan's frantic cry sounded through a roar that came suddenly to fill the brick-walled room with muffled thunder. Operator 5 spun to see a torrent of water cascading, boiling white, to the floor. It was pouring from the end of a thick pipe, twelve inches across, protruding into the room just beneath the ceiling. It washed across the floor, flooding about V-44's still form, churning under the power of the downpour.

Z-7 had paused just behind Operator 5. Now he whirled

toward the door. He found the way closed. While Jimmy Christopher swung again to cover Bord, Z-7 flung himself against the panels. Twice he crashed his shoulder against it; then, breathlessly, he drew back.

"That door is steel! It's watertight!"

Above the sill, the water was flooding. Jimmy Christopher turned quickly, saw that there was no other opening in the room—none other than the huge pipe from which the swift cascade was plunging. He thrust his gun hard against Bord's chest, reached for the lever which the espionage agent had shifted. He thrust it back to its first position.

Still the water torrented down into the room. Still the heavy door remained firmly shut. Bord uttered a low, triumphant laugh. "You will not get out! We have seen to that! You will stay here to drown!"

Operator 5 stood erect, his dark eyes glinting into those of the foreign agent. Already the water was rising coldly about his ankles. The room shook with the dull roar of the pouring stream. It was small but the volume of water sluicing into it was lifting the level rapidly. Above spread a flat ceiling to which the surface would rise until the entire room was filled.

A death-trap!

Bord laughed evilly again. "Yes, we have seen to that! One throw of the lever opens the vent and closes the door. The circuit breaks so that the lever does not control it again. Once the door is shut, you can do nothing to open it, nothing to stop the water! I—I know how to escape, but you will never get out!"

JIMMY CHRISTOPHER stepped forward grimly. The

123

cold water lapped halfway to his knees as he searched Bord. His crisp command brought Z-7 to cover the secret agent while he spun to Tim Donovan. He sliced the keen blade of a pocket-knife against the boy's bonds.

Wide-eyed, breathing hard, the Irish lad tore himself free. "Gee, Jimmy! It's my fault!"

"Okay, Tim!" Jimmy Christopher answered wryly. "Take Z-7's gun and keep that man covered. If he starts to make another move, stop him with a bullet—take no chances. Chief! Get at that door!"

The anxious boy snatched the automatic from the Washington chief, grimly confronted the leering Bord. Z-7 turned again to the water-tight door. He snatched up a chair, drove it sharply against the panels. At the first blow its legs cracked off. Z-7 crashed it down again and again; when he stepped back, the chair was in fragments. The door was scarcely scarred—and the water had risen to his knees.

Operator 5 had turned quickly to the wireless equipment on the table. The snap of a switch had brought a glow to the warming tubes. He turned back to see Z-7 desperately attacking the door with a second chair. Eyes narrowed, he faced the triumphant Bord, who shouted: "I will get out, but you will not!"

"Perhaps," Jimmy Christopher declared through the roar of the torrent. "We won't argue. You were about to receive a wireless message. I'll transcribe it for you."

Bord's eyes flickered dangerously as Operator 5 bent over the shortwave receiver, fitted 'phones to his ears, noted the settings of the dials but did not touch them. He felt sure the set was already tuned to the secretly-used wave-band. He brought pad and paper close, waited while the water crept higher above his knees—waited while he pressed the 'phones close to hear any faint signal through the thunder of the torrent….

"Ten minutes!" Bord screamed. "Ten minutes and the last of the air will be gone—the water will be at the ceiling. You do not see the air-vents? There they are! You will drown like rats and the world will not know! But I will get out—I will get out!"

Operator 5 still bent alertly over the table. Into the 'phones sang a high-pitched, sputtering note. From some faraway transmitter, a signal was flashing into the receiver. Intently he listened past the roar of the rising water. Swiftly he scribbled apparently meaningless letters on the pad:

wghysa f i nkatnefigbxw pllaordiqvy tiam idwbp xjiwhrbqz—

Bord blurted: "The message is coming in? It will mean nothing to you! You cannot decipher it! We have planned too well for you—too well!"

OVER THE table Jimmy Christopher bent, concentrating on the sputtering oscillator note. Tim Donovan stood motionless while the lapping water washed up to his chest. The level was mounting, and once the water penetrated the receiver, the apparatus would cease to function. Swiftly Operator 5's pencil scratched:

—josfucht aocyqmt zuap hquy vgts kiarc

The singing in the 'phones stopped. Z-7 peered haggardly at Jimmy Christopher. Tim Donovan raised the automatic above

"Ten minutes!" Bord screamed. "Ten minutes and the last of the air will be gone! The water will be at the ceiling!"

the mounting level of the chopping water. It was washing upon the table now. The signals resumed as Operator 5 waited. A swift repetition of the code message began coming through. Only half the words had sounded before a wave lapped into the condensers.

"I compliment you, Bord," Jimmy Christopher said quietly. "You have planned well."

"Too well for you!" the espionage agent gloated. "It won't be long now till the water reaches the ceiling. The message—what good does it do you now? It is to tell me where the next shell will fall at midnight, but that you shall never know!"

"You begin to convince me," Jimmy Christopher answered.

"You may well believe! Nothing can stop that water coming in now—nothing but a valve located far from this room! The door was closed by a motor and now a powerful magnet is holding it in place. The magnet is in contact with the steel of the door and it is strong enough that forty men could not push it open!"

Light glittered in Operator 5's dark eyes. "For that information, Bord," he declared, "I am most grateful!"

Bord's triumphant smile vanished as Jimmy Christopher peered at the bright globes burning overhead. He turned quickly. Groping beneath the whipping surface, dragged the radio table to the center of the floor. He climbed on it, readied—but the globes were beyond his fingers. Imperatively he called down: "Chief, cover Bord! Tim—up here, quick!"

The boy groped through neck-high water. He dragged himself upon the table, coat streaming. Jimmy Christopher thrust the pocket-knife into his hand as he shuddered with the cold. "Follow directions, Tim! I'll lift you. Unscrew one of those bulbs, and stick at knife into the socket. Quick, old-timer! It's our only chance! Shove that knife in, Tim!"

INTO THE socket, the boy thrust the blade. A spiteful spark snapped. Instantly, the other globes winked out. Utter darkness filled the crypt—blackness torn by the roar of the rising water.

Operator 5 lowered Tim Donovan to the table. He leaped toward the door, ducked low into the tearing currents. While his breath burned in his lungs, he struggled to brace himself against the brick floor, to thrust all his weight against the door. The swirling force of the water played upon him as he exerted all his strength. His heart pounded with pain. A breath was becoming an excruciating necessity when—suddenly the door yielded!

Water rushed through, flooding into the black crypts beyond. Jimmy Christopher was flung aside by the outpour, clung to the jamb. From the roaring darkness, Z-7's voice warned Bord sharply: "Don't move!"

As the first power of the spilling water subsided, Operator 5 stepped back, brought from his pocket a small electric torch. A gleam flickered as he touched the button. It swept across Tim Donovan, just inside the door. The rush had torn the boy from the table, flung him against the wall. Z-7, lashing in the foam, was struggling with one arm hooked about Bord's neck. The secret agent twisted violently as the light turned upon him, struck a blow that staggered the Washington chief. He tore loose and leaped away.

"No farther!" Jimmy Christopher's command stopped the spy short. His wet automatic twinkled in the gleam, leveled at

Bord's heart. Z-7, gasping, struggled through the door while water churned around his knees. Tim Donovan lurched through and seized Operator 5's left arm.

"I'd hate to have to kill you, Bord," Jimmy Christopher growled.

The secret agent's glistening face was pale as death. Z-7's gun pressed hard against his back. Tim Donovan peered at the knife he still gripped in one hard fist, gasped: "Jimmy! Gee, I thought we couldn't get out of there! How—how'd you do it, Jimmy?"

Operator 5 peered grimly at Bord as he answered. "Our host was too proud of his work. He betrayed himself by mentioning the magnet that held the steel door closed. I took a chance the magnet was operated by the same current that connected with the lights. When you pushed the knife into the socket, Tim, you short-circuited the line and blew the fuse. All that was left to do was to overcome the residual force of the magnet. That may not be the way our host planned to get out—but it worked!"

"It sure did, Jimmy!" the Irish lad exclaimed admiringly.

"I think that now," Operator 5 continued quietly, "our host will become our guest—at M-11!"

CHAPTER 8
THE COMET STRIKES AGAIN

NEWSBOYS WERE still shouting the terrifying news of the Chicago blast when, an hour later, Operator 5 and Tim Donovan opened the entrance beside the establishment of Marielle which led into Headquarters M-11. They had brought their prisoner immediately to the secret suite; they had left and changed into dry clothing. On their return they code-worded their way to Z-7's inner office.

The Washington chief rose quickly as they entered. He had also changed clothing and returned to M-11. His face was gaunt and dark-lined as a result of the nerve-straining, sleep-denying demands of his duty. He gripped Jimmy Christopher's hand wryly as he said: "I'm exhausted enough to drop, but you seem fresh as ever! The Secretary of State has just communicated with us. He informs us that the Ambassador from the Court of St. James has demanded an explanation of the newspaper reports blaming England for the attacks upon us. This has caused an extremely delicate international crisis."

Jimmy Christopher answered briskly: "Chief, there is only one way to escape the danger of war. That is to locate and destroy the big gun that is firing upon us."

Z-7 moaned. "But we still have made no headway. Here," and he flipped a flimsy, "is another report from our headquarters. No explosion such as a big gun makes was heard anywhere in the country at noon. It must be located far from any populated center but—we're completely at a loss!"

Operator 5 sat alertly at his desk. "Have any of our New York agents reported a suspicious penthouse that might be the head-quarters of Radi Havara?"

"So far, no!"

Jimmy Christopher tipped a cam of the Dictaphone, touched a button that opened a line to the codes—and ciphers-room of

M-11. Quickly he asked: "Are you still working on the short-wave message?"

"We are, sir, but we haven't begun to crack it yet. It's one of the most difficult we've ever tackled. Even with the code-book we—"

"Bring it here at once!" Of Z-7, Operator 5 asked: "Is Bord here now?"

"Yes; but so far, like V-44, he refuses absolutely to talk. We know now, thank God, that Urakia is behind these attacks. Bord is typical of the Urakian patriots, the kind of man who has caused his country to be called the Bulldog of Europe. The Japanese and Chinese are no more loyal—no more self-sacrificing—than they."

"I want Bord brought to this office at once." As Z-7 spoke through the Dictaphone relaying the message, Operator 5 thoughtfully fingered his death-charm. "We have cleared away all doubt as to the motive behind these attacks, Chief. We have brought our enemy into the light. Yet even that may be no advantage to us if—"

A knock sounded; the door opened. A man who peered through thick eyeglasses, who looked like a wizened professor—one of the keenest of the cryptogram experts at M-11—brought to Operator 5's desk a thin book and the intercepted wireless message.

"We have not yet been able to discover what type it is, sir," he explained, crestfallen. "It may be unsolvable. Our copy of the Urakian code-book has proved of no value."

"I'll tackle it."

IMMEDIATELY THE cipher expert left the door opened again. The espionage agent named Bord came into the office. He had been given dry clothing which fitted him tightly. He glared defiance at Jimmy Christopher as he strode forward.

Operator 5 picked up the leather-covered book that had been brought in by the cipher expert. "Here," he said, "is a copy of all codes used by the Urakian government. It has been in our possession for months—it is only one example of how efficiently our system functions."

"Even with that book you will not find the secret of that message!"

"Perhaps...." Jimmy Christopher's gaze held steadily on Bord's deep-set eyes. "We are well aware of the motive behind your tactics. You, under the direction of Radi Havara, have let it be known that a shell will explode somewhere in this country every twelve hours, exactly on the dot of noon and midnight. The certainty that it *will* fall, coupled with the uncertainty of *where* it will fall—is calculated to arouse terror among our people. I compliment you that you are succeeding."

Bord snarled, his eyes blazing: "We have only begun! Your discovering our secret will not hinder us! Great Britain is to blame in the minds of your people and the fury of the mob cannot be stilled once it is directed against a foe! The people will force your government into war to avenge these atrocities— they will demand that war be declared before the shells fall on your defenses: the Panamá Canal, your coast artillery units, your navy ships, your army camps—before you are rendered utterly defenseless!"

"But," Operator 5 answered quietly, "the secret of where the next shell will fall is in this message."

"I defy you to solve it!" Jimmy Christopher drew pencil and pad close grimly. He studied the cabalistic words in silence. He turned from page to page of the Urakian code-book while Bord's eyes blazed confident defiance. While he worked, Z-7 strode close to the secret agent.

"Your government," he declared, "knows very well that the next European war will spell annihilation for it. Every nation in Europe is being drawn into the most terrible war the world has ever known. In such a war, the rights and securities of neutral countries such as Urakia will cease to exist. Your government will have to ally itself with greater powers—fight for its life. If it does not do that, it will perish. You know that! That is what you are striving—by the most devilish scheme ever devised—to avoid!"

"Say what you will!" Bord exclaimed. "Americans believe the enemy is Great Britain. You will go to war with Great Britain Urakia will escape the crush of a European war!"

Operator 5 raised shining eyes to Bord's flushed face. "I see," he said quietly, "that our cipher experts have had great difficulty because they have overlooked the time element in this message.* I luckily noted the exact time this message came in.

* AUTHOR'S NOTE: An example of the importance of the time element in certain cipher systems are the United States navy codes used during the World War. When long messages were sent, cipher shifted to cipher with the passage of time. Translators had to have the exact Greenwich Mean

Chief—It's a reversed clock cipher, and the rest is easy. I'll have it in a moment!"

Bord stared, blurted: "Impossible!"

OPERATOR 5 wrote rapidly. "A reversed clock code, yes— to avoid repetition of letters—to bring about false repetitions! It's coming!" The pencil-point flew as Z-7 strode to the desk, as Bord half rose with unbounded astonishment. On the pad words appeared:

Advice R H transmitted accordingly next shell—

"It will avail you nothing!" Bord screamed. "Even if you know, the shell will come!"

"Chief!" Jimmy Christopher jerked from his chair, his eyes glittering, his lips pinched hard. Z-7 whirled to him in alarm. His voice crackled: "Get the Secretary of War on the wire at once! The Secretary himself—no other!"

Z-7 snatched at the completed message. His face went pale. He read again, amazed, the last words of the translation:

—scheduled midnight tonight will fall West Point.

The Washington chief spun to the door of the communications-room. He snapped orders at the dispatcher at the desk. The agent at the switchboard swiftly began making connections over special lines connecting with the Capital. Z-7 turned back to exclaim: "West Point! God—there are almost fourteen hundred

Time a message was sent in order to know which code to begin translating. Lacking this key, the message was undecipherable.

cadets there now—youngsters! A shell falling into the Military Academy is certain to kill hundreds of them! It's not possible that such a terrible blow—"

"Only too possible, Chief!" Operator 5 broke in. "The sinking of the *Lusitania* did much to throw us into the World War. It wasn't an American ship—it was known to be carrying contraband—but its destruction aroused our people. The shelling of West Point—the killing of hundreds of cadets by an enemy gun—will have a far more powerful effect. The Urakian government is doing everything possible to drive us into war!"

Again Bord half-rose as the communications-door snapped open. The chief-dispatcher exclaimed: "Operator 5, the Secretary of War is on the wire!"

Jimmy Christopher snatched up the desk instrument. He peered intently at the espionage agent as he talked. "Mr. Secretary, Operator 5 calling. I have just uncovered an appalling piece of information. It must be acted upon without a moment's delay. The United States Military Academy at West Point is under your direct jurisdiction. It is necessary that you order it evacuated at once."

"Order—In God's name—why?"

"Because the next shell, due to fall at exactly midnight, Eastern Standard Time, will hit the Academy. Unless the cadets are removed before then, it will mean hundreds of deaths. It is not the loss of life alone which must be avoided, but the effect such a disaster would have on our people. Transmit imperative orders to the West Point staff at once! Every human being must be out of the Academy by midnight. I suggest that you order them removed to Fort Totten. Every man, without exception, must leave West Point. Any who stays is as good as dead!"

Operator 5 lowered the 'phone, turned darkened eyes upon the foreign espionage agent. Bord had risen from his chair. His eyes were blazing with defiant triumph. He spoke thickly, heatedly—words that struck Z-7 motionless, chilled Jimmy Christopher's heart:

"It will do no good! Our agents are watching West Point even now! They will report the movement of the cadets! The shell will follow! If they go to Fort Totten, the shell will fall there! If they go to any other place it will also find them! Without fail, that projectile will search them out—*at midnight tonight!*"

AT FORT TOTTEN, at College Point, New York, a short distance down the Hudson from the famed Military Academy, there was an air of tense suspense. The Headquarters of the Second Coast Artillery district presented an unparalleled scene. West Point cadets, in smart uniforms and great coats, crowded over the snow-covered greensward and the parade grounds. Officers paced back and forth nervously, peering at the sky. Tension—nerve-rawing tension—rose suddenly to an unbearable pitch by the drone of motors in the sky.

Out of the darkness, a plane swooped low, followed by a second. Their wing-lights streaked colored circles as they banked to land. They swung down upon the parade-ground and shuttled to its edge. Officers hurried toward them.

From the control pit of the first—an army pursuit from Mitchell Field—Operator 5 climbed. He turned to peer at the man in the second cubby—the square-faced, evil-eyed agent named Bord. He inspected the handcuffs that linked Bord to the cowling. He turned briskly toward the passengers of the second plane.

Z-7 and Tim Donovan stopped anxiously at Jimmy Christopher's side. "Great Scott!" exclaimed the Washington chief, glancing at his wrist-watch. "There is little enough time!"

"Enough, Chief," Jimmy Christopher answered. He turned again to the officers who stopped near him.

He recognized the ruddy features of Major-General Rodman MacBride, Chief Staff, Army. Beside him stood members of the West Point staff and Major General Arthur Whitney, Chief of Coast Artillery. Acting Commander Hugh Pitman, lean and spare, advanced with General MacBride.

"We have been expecting you," the Army Chief of Staff, said quietly. "The Secretary of War has just advised me by telephone to execute any orders you give."

"I have orders to be acted upon immediately," Operator 5 answered. "Fort Totten is to be evacuated at the soonest possible moment."

General MacBride blurted: "What? We have just—"

"Every man," Jimmy Christopher insisted, "is to leave this fort without delay. Instruct them to scatter—anywhere they please—and not return until after midnight. There is not a moment to waste!"

Major General MacBride's wrist-watch gleamed. "You believe—"

"The shell will fall here instead of at West Point. The evacuation of West Point could not be kept secret. Enemy spies have reported to the crew of the hidden big gun that all cadets and officers have transferred. That gun is training on this fort this very moment. At midnight the shell will come—and there are very few minutes left!"

Commander Pitman protested: "In God's name—if that's true, why were we not given these orders sooner? There is scarcely time—"

"Orders were not given sooner," Operator 5 answered swiftly, "because it is necessary for this second evacuation to take place so that the commander of the hidden cannon can be informed of it by his spies. That shell will fall somewhere, I promise you. Let it strike here then. Let this fort by emptied as swiftly as possible. Gentlemen—issue those orders at once!"

THE OFFICERS whirled, ran toward the operations-office. Their snapping words carried commands to others officers hurrying near. These in turn raced across the grounds to spread the alarm to every scattered point. Through the darkness of the night the warning flashed.

"Evacuate at once! Every man out of the fort! Go anywhere—but get out!"

Jimmy Christopher turned grimly to peer again at the spy, Bord, who was huddling in the back pit of his waiting plane. He spoke quietly to Z-7.

"Into the air, Chief! Avoid a position directly above this field. Hold yourself ready to land immediately after the shell falls. Tim—you're going with Z-7, old-timer."

The Irish lad's eyes widened anxiously. "Gee, Jimmy—you're going up right away, too? It's almost midnight!"

"I know, Tim—but I'm staying. Perhaps I'll have time to get away before it hits—I'm not sure. If I don't—"

Jimmy Christopher's voice trailed away at a thought he could not voice. Z-7 tugged at the tough Irish lad's arm, urged him away. Operator 5 stood motionless, watching Tim and the Washington chief climb into the other waiting plane. The prop slashed swiftly; the trucks rolled across tramped snow. Jimmy Christopher's dark eyes followed as it rushed across the parade ground, swooped into the sky.

He turned again to see a growing crowd massing away toward the gates. His imperative orders were being swiftly carried out. Word had flashed to every man.

Operator 5 glanced at the glowing dial of his watch. White-shining hands were indicating two minutes of twelve. He peered into Bord's dark face and spoke:

"You and I," he said, "are facing a showdown, Bord. So far you have refused us all information. You have spoken no word to reveal the location of the big gun, nor the whereabouts of Radi Havara. Now it lacks exactly two minutes of midnight—and perhaps, within those two minutes, you will decide to speak."

Bord blurted: "I will tell you nothing!"

"We will wait here together, Bord," Jimmy Christopher drawled, "until you reveal those secrets."

Bord's gaze jerked skyward. When he looked down again, quickly, into Operator 5's grim face. His eyes glinted with fear. "Wait—here?"

"On this very spot, where the shell will fall. You have assured me that it will strike this fort!"

140

OPERATOR 5 seized the cowling of the fore-pit, swung over to the seat. The shining dial of his wrist-watch gleamed again as he raised it.

"Bord, the shell is coming even now. It is tearing through the sky, high in the stratosphere, at this every moment. It is streaking toward this field, flying down at us—now!"

Bord stared in terror. "I know nothing to tell you! You cannot trick me. You will not dare to stay!"

"We will stay," Operator 5 declared levelly, "until you speak—until that shell smashes down on us!"

Bord's eyes peered frantically into Operator 5's face. In the darkness, the gleam of the wristwatch was bright. Jimmy Christopher peered across the grounds, saw that the last of the men were crowding through the gates, mobbing out along the roads. Overhead, the drone of an airplane sounded—the ship carrying Z-7 and Tim Donovan, circling slowly through the gloom. The motor of the plane on the field clicked over as Jimmy Christopher peered into the zenith.

"It is coming, Bord! Coming now—closer and closer! The explosion will tear you to small pieces unless you speak. There is still time, Bord—but there is less than a minute left to—"

Into Operator 5's words cut the first whining cry of the descending shell!

Jimmy Christopher turned low-lidded eyes skyward. Bord tensed up in the second cubby, tugging frantically at the cuffs which pinioned him. The note of the falling shell rose swiftly to a scream that loudened with each tick of Operator 5's wrist-watch. Sharper and more powerful, the sound pierced the night....

141

Bord blurted, "God—God!"

High in the zenith, the first streak of light appeared. The comet of doom flashed out of the depths of the night. Growing swiftly to white hotness, it cut its brilliant path downward—directly overhead. Instant by instant it flashed closer—plunging toward the very heart of Fort Totten, toward the black plane waiting on the field.

"Bord! Before it is too late—!"

Bord recoiled, his hands fluttering, his eyes shining with a mad light, cringing under the loudening wail of the falling shell. "For the sake of God! I'll tell you! Fly off this field now—*now!* I swear I'll tell you—!"

"The gun, Bord!" Jimmy Christopher shouted through the scream of the shell. "Where is it? Where is Radi Havara?"

"The gun—I do not know!" Bord screamed. "I'll tell you where the woman is! For the sake of God! I swear—I'll tell you everything!"

Operator 5 twisted swiftly to the controls. He threw off the brakes, his eyes shining with triumph, jammed the throttle wide open. As the ship rolled swiftly across the tracked snow, he peered at the blinding light streaking down from above. Even through the snarl of the motor, the shrill wail pierced. The plane rushed at the limit of its power—sped into the vibrating darkness.

It slashed up, wings rocking. It drove straight, rising swiftly. Operator 5 crouched to the controls while Bord twisted to stare in speechless horror at the lengthening streak in the sky—a streak that reached swiftly to touch the field. Then the shell struck!

TERRIFIC, RENDING power blasted out of the night. A gigantic spray of fire flashed, reaching high, flashing its light of doom through thick, rolling clouds of fumes. The gargantuan power of the impact shook all the earth and the sky as a crater tore deep—as flying fragments of the burst shell hissed far. The air churned violently with the force of the explosion, whipping the plane that was launching even then beyond the limits of the fort.

In the swift, savage air-currents, Operator 5's crate lurched and swung. He gripped the stick, steadied the rudder, nerves hot and tight, muscles reacting instantaneously to the wrenching of the wind. Through the air around him ragged steel fragments whistled. They ripped through the fuselage, slashed through the wings. One gashed Operator 5's coat-sleeve as he fought to keep the plane in the air. Through a chaotic cyclone he flung his crate, through darkness thickened with clouding, choking fumes.

High above him sounded the drone of the plane carrying Z-7 and Tim Donovan. He noted the great black patch where the snow had vanished—where the shell had struck. Buildings were crumpled; stone walls had vanished. Two gigantic gun abutments were now crumbled masses of cement burying toppled cannons. Disaster had struck devastatingly across the grounds.

Grimly, Jimmy Christopher whirled down toward a far section of the parade grounds. Upthrown earth there blackened the snow and made landing precarious. He slashed low, easing back the throttle, while he heard the other plane follow. Trucks bumped over masses of loose earth as he drew the brakes hard.

He hopped from the fore-pit, reached into the rear one to grip Bord's arms. While he dragged the foreign agent up, the second plane stopped; Z-7 and Tim Donovan scrambled from it. They ran frantically toward Operator 5, through air still thick with fumes.

"I'm okay, Tim!" Operator 5 yelled. "Chief—help me with Bord! He's hurt!"

Together, they raised the spy from the rear pit. Bord's head lolled, dripping red. Behind the right ear, his scalp was gashed by a flying fragment of shell. He sagged limply, unconscious, as Jimmy Christopher supported him and peered into his death-white face.

"Chief, we've got to get him to a hospital right away! He'll talk now! Our only chance, Chief—our only chance!"

THE SPOTLESS hospital room was silent. On the bed Bord lay, his head bandaged, his eyes open and staring blankly at the ceiling. He lay lax, unmoving, his face an expressionless mask.

He had been rushed into New York by car after Operator 5 had given him first aid. Z-7 had called Dr. Morton Hendricks, one of the ablest surgeons in the city. Dr. Hendricks bent over Bord now, a light flashing in his hand, testing the reflexes of Bord's eyes. He straightened, wagging his head.

Z-7 asked quickly: "Is he seriously injured? Will he live?"

Operator 5 listened intently to the answer. "The scalp wound is not serious. There is no danger that he will die. Yet, the shock has affected his mind. His, gentlemen, is a case of hyper amnesia. His memory has ceased to function. He can recall nothing that he has formerly known."

Jimmy Christopher declared: "Dr. Hendricks, it is absolutely imperative that his memory function again—if it is humanly possible!"

"I will do my best, but—" The great surgeon shrugged.

Z-7 exclaimed: "This man has information that we must have. He alone can give it to us. You must do everything possible to restore his memory! Can you give us any assurance—?"

"No. These cases are most difficult. It may be years before this man's memory returns, or it may never function again at all. I can promise you nothing. I can only try...."

Grimly Operator 5 peered at the blank, lightless eyes of the agent Bord—and was silent....

CHAPTER 9
MIND OVER MIND

THE DOORMAN of the staid apartment-house in the East Sixties of Manhattan bowed to the brisk-mannered young man who strode from a taxi: "Good evening, Mr. Walsh."

"Good evening," Jimmy Christopher returned.

He left the elevator at the eleventh floor. With a key of which no duplicate existed, he opened a door of mahogany veneer over toughest steel. He strode into the adjoining bedroom, swung a strange contrivance toward the window.

On an anchored table sat a device consisting of a drum around which a rope-ladder was coiled, a ratchet, an electric motor, and a black box like a camera affixed to a flexible gooseneck. Operator 5 opened the window and swung the box outward over the sill. He uncoiled forty feet of the ladder, let it snake into the darkness outside. He climbed out upon it.

He descended the ladder into a well of darkness separating the apartment-house from the next. He swung to a balcony, drew his torch from his pocket, and flashed a beam upward. Striking the lens in the black box, it actuated a photoelectric cell which in turn closed a relay. The rope ladder coiled upward; the window slid shut uncannily. Operator 5 stepped from the balcony, walked through an apartment, entered a hallway, and angled to another door.

In this way, Jimmy Christopher threw off any possible shadower.

He touched a call-button inscribed *Carleton Victor*, and the door was opened by a cool-faced manservant who greeted him with: "Good evening, Mr. Victor."

"Good evening, Crowe."

Crowe, gentleman's gentleman extraordinary, assisted Carleton Victor from his top-coat, took his hat and cane. He did not suspect that his master was the undercover ace of America. Crowe accepted him as what he appeared to be—a creative artist in photography, who maintained sumptuous studios on Fifth Avenue. None of the clients who came to the renowned studio—world famous statesmen, society leaders, dignitaries, industrial magnates—suspected any more than Crowe that

Carleton Victor was a convenient blind to mask the secret activities of Operator 5.

"You have, I trust, Crowe," Victor said quietly, "remained indoors and not ventured upon the streets?"

"Quite, sir."

"That is wise, Crowe. You would not fare well if you happened to be about when another shell fell into New York."

Crowe blinked. "Shell, sir? I don't believe I understand, sir."

Victor's eyebrows arched. "Crowe, it is possible that you know nothing of the terrific explosions in Times Square, and in Chicago, and just a short while ago at Fort Totten?"

"Explosions? No, sir! You see, sir, I never read the newspapers. Has something serious happened, Mr. Victor?"

"You had best," Carleton Victor said enigmatically, "not trouble your mind about it, Crowe. Proceed along the even tenor of your ways. I quite envy you your peace of mind."

"Yes, sir?" Crowe said, and blinked in bewilderment as Victor stepped into a closet opening off the vestibule.

THE CLOSET was sound-proofed; it contained nothing save a telephone and a chair. The instrument was connected with a special line which Carleton Victor never used. Behind this door, the artist in photography vanished and Operator 5 again came into being. He lifted the receiver, called the secret number of Intelligence Headquarters M-11. A voice said: "Eden Theatre."

"The box office, please."

"The box-office is closed."

"The projection booth, then."

Signals exchanged, Operator 5 touched a cam protruding through the wall. It shunted into the line a frequency distorter which made eavesdropping impossible. Speaking quietly, he asked for Z-7. Immediately the Washington chief answered.

"Has Dr. Hendricks any report, Chief?"

"None! Bord's mind is still a complete blank. It's a devilish trick of fate. The one man who could give us an invaluable lead— and he is unable to remember any of the information we want!"

Jimmy Christopher declared bitterly: "Then we can only wait. What report from our direction-finders, Chief? Have they charted the wireless message Bord was to receive this afternoon?"

"Yes, but the lines do not converge anywhere within the United States. The message evidently came from Europe, but at such distance that the direction-finders are not accurate enough to locate the sending station precisely. Another lead—gone!

"Further reports, Operator 5, leave us completely in the dark. Radi Havara has not been seen, nor her headquarters located. Nor was explosion like that of a big gun was heard anywhere in the United States at midnight. Fortunately, thanks to you, although terrific damage was done at Fort Totten, not a single man was hurt or killed. But in the meantime, serious international complications are arising.

"We have just received a code message from K-6 in London, and another from D-9 in Paris, which substantiate each other. Rumors are again flying through European diplomatic circles of a secret alliance between Great Britain and Japan.* The news must be taken seriously—it is of grave consequence.

"It will heighten the wave of terror gripping this country now. The people will read into it the meaning that England is ready to make war against us by allying itself with another nation distinctly unfriendly to us now. Britain on the East— Japan on the West! It lends weight to all the bitterness that has been aroused as a result of the economic struggle between us and those two countries. Think of it! It will stir our people into a demand for war. Coupled with the shell attacks, it will make war inevitable,—especially when the statement recently made by General Sato is remembered!" **

OPERATOR 5 disconnected; Carleton Victor stepped from the soundproofed closet. Crowe followed him into the spacious bedroom; he assisted his master with a change of clothing. Knotting an exquisite cravat, Victor saw the manservant eyeing him

---

* AUTHOR'S NOTE: The rumor of an Anglo-Japanese alliance first reached the United States through foreign newspaper correspondents on August 29, 1934. Walter Duranty, famed representative of the *New York Times*, in a special cable sent from Moscow on August 28, stated in his report:

"… A section of British opinion and the Conservative British press is… anti-American, decidedly anti-Russian and pro-Japanese."

** AUTHOR'S NOTE: Recently Lieutenant-General Kiakatsu Sato, retired, of the Japanese Imperial Army, was quoted as having declared:

"It is our duty to detest and loathe the people of the United States. There is no need to employ honey-coated words or high-sounding expressions. We must speak out frankly, without reserve. Our enemy is the United States of

with mild curiosity. "I fear, sir, that you are not getting your proper rest."

"I fear, Crowe, that you're right! I am, shall I say, very busy."

"Creating your works of art, I am sure, is very demanding and very tiring."

"Very, Crowe!" Victor said wryly.

The manservant helped him again with top-coat and derby. At the outer door, Victor paused, glancing back at him. He said quietly: "Don't wait up for me, Crowe. I may be late—very late. In fact, if I do not return within a week, I suggest that you find yourself another position. There are letters of recommendation—very high recommendation, Crowe—in the desk."

"But, sir! I am quite happy here. I do not care to serve another gentleman, sir. If I am not satisfactory to you, of course—"

"You are, Crowe," Victor said softly, "a joy to me. I suggest this only because—because, Crowe, I may not return at all!"

America. Arise! Exert yourselves! Prepare for the coming Japanese-American war! We must chastise our enemy, the United States of America!"

A prominent editorial writer of Tokyo has also been quoted as declaring, in regard to the people of the United States:

"Whatever may be their object, their actions are more despicable than those of the Germans, whose atrocities they attacked as being worthy of the Huns. At least these Americans are barbarians who are on a lower plane of civilization than we Japanese."

In this connection it is significant to note that during the budget year of 1934–35; Japan is admittedly spending 13,814,000 yen (more than four million dollars) upon its organizations of secret combat.

He dosed the door and Crowe stood blinking—blinking as his coolish, aristocratic face slowly turned white....

A TAXI carried Jimmy Christopher to a brownstone house in the East Forties of Manhattan which was the home of his father—in the records of the Intelligence Service, Address Y. When a key admitted him, Tim Donovan bounded down the stairs. The boy gripped Operator 5's arm eagerly. "Di's here! Dad's been waiting for you, too. Jimmy—got a new trick to show me?"

"That must wait, Tim, I'm afraid."

Operator 5 strode into the quiet living room as Diane Elliot hurried toward him. She flung her arms around his neck and kissed him full on the lips. The warmth of her greeting brought a hot flush to his face as she backed away laughing.

"Facing a gun doesn't bother you at all, Jimmy Christopher— but a kiss upsets you completely!"

"*Your* kiss, Di," Operator 5 smiled, and turned quickly to the quiet-mannered man who came from a deep chair with hand out-reached. "Dad!"

John Christopher, once designated Operator Q-6 in the United States Intelligence Service, had been forced to abandon his strenuous duties following the infliction of a serious wound. Two bullets still lay so close to his heart that no surgeon dared attempt to remove them, and a life of quiet was forced upon him. He gloried in the achievement of his son, finding there a sense of accomplishment otherwise denied him. His hand-clasp was warm and firm. "Headway, Jimmy?"

"Very little, Dad," Operator 5 said. "I'm trying my best, but—"

"Nonsense, Jimmy Christopher!" Diane interrupted. "You're getting results far greater than you imagine—and you've got plenty of ideas that you don't hint to anyone. You're getting ready to act, and act fast. I know all the signs!"

Operator 5 smiled. "I only hope," he said quietly, "that I can justify the trust placed in me. Every twelve hours multiplies the danger of this situation. War closing down upon us. It's a horrible thing—and still that big gun is hidden beyond our reach."

Operator 5 threw off coat and hat, strode quickly into the rear rooms which he had outfitted as his work-shop. They were filled with devices, the nature of some of which only Jimmy Christopher knew. While Tim Donovan watched eagerly, he set to work.

At the woodworking bench, he quickly fashioned a block to which he affixed a pedestal a few inches high. From a case he brought an enclosed electric motor of the universal type, and this he mounted on the top of the pedestal. When he had connected a cord and plug to the motor, he turned to a bench and worked again upon a device which Tim Donovan could not fathom. Completed, it was a small rimless wheel, with four spokes, to each of which was affixed a small round mirror. Operator 5 tightened a set-screw which fastened it firmly to the shaft of the motor. When he finished, the device looked somewhat like an electric fan with the mirrored spokes replacing the blades. He tested it, and the mirrors whirled out a blaze of light. He placed it in a box and brought it into the living-room.

OPERATOR 5 glanced at his wristwatch, looked up to see Tim Donovan still eyeing him eagerly.

"Okay, old-timer," he smiled. "There may be time for a new trick. Wait here a minute—and prepare to be completely fooled."

"Gee, Jimmy—that's swell! Is that apparatus you just made part of it?"

"That, Tim, is for a far different purpose," Jimmy Christopher answered as he stepped back into the workrooms.

When he returned a moment later he was carrying a tray on which rested a small glass half filled with water. He extended it toward Tim Donovan while Diane and John Christopher watched smilingly.

"Take it, Tim. Taste it to make sure it's just plain water. Satisfied? Now, place it on the palm of my left hand—and watch!"

Putting the tray aside, Jimmy Christopher allowed the small glass to rest on his left palm with the fingers of that hand extended. He brought his right hand over the glass, cupped it, and appeared to press hard.

"It's melting, Tim!" he exclaimed. "The glass is vanishing and the water is evaporating. See now—my two palms are touching! Presto!—it's gone entirely!"

Operator 5 separated his hands, fingers spread wide apart, displayed them quite empty before the astounded Irish lad. Tim immediately seized Jimmy Christopher's hands but could find nothing concealed in them. He backed away completely baffled.

"Gee, I don't see how you could do that, Jimmy! It was a real glass and real water, and you couldn't've just slipped it away somewhere. How'd you do it?"

Operator 5 glanced at his watch, then said quickly:

"I'll explain it, Tim—and then I've got to make an important call. That trick was accomplished by a tried and true device known to all magicians, one of the old stand-bys like the false thumb-tip I've already shown you how to use.* It is called a 'pull,' and it's extremely simple. Look at this!"

Operator 5 quickly removed his coat and vest. To the back of the vest was fastened the device called a "pull." It was simply a length of black elastic, to one end of which was knotted a safety-pin, and to the other end, in this case, a large but ordinary cork to which the vanished glass of water was adhering. Tim's eyes rounded with astonishment as the secret was revealed.

"All pulls consist of an elastic, a pin, and one of several different devices on the lower end. The device may be a thin shell into which a silk handkerchief can be stuffed, or a small tube to hold a cigarette. In use, the pin is fastened under the coat or up the sleeve so that the empty pull hangs out of sight. When the device is brought into use, the rubber is stretched. Once the pull is released, it flies out of sight, and the object disappears.

"This special pull, Tim, is easily made. It is, you see, a large cork, just the right size to fit into this small glass. It goes in only an inch or so, not to the level of the water. All you need to do is to get a small glass and a cork to fit—then, drill a hole through the center of the cork from top to bottom and tighten an eye-bolt through it. Attach the elastic and the safety pin, and you're all set.

---

* AUTHOR'S NOTE: In each of the Operator 5 narratives, Jimmy Christopher has presented and explained one or more feats of legerdemain which he originates or perfects in his work-shop. They are simple, effective, and based upon fundamental principles of the art of magic.

"**WHEN I** came out to begin this trick, the pin was fastened at a point on the back of my vest so that when the pull was released it would hang just out of sight under the tail of my coat. I had already placed the cork in my right trouser pocket. While you were sipping the water, I brought the pull into my right hand, and you did not notice the perfectly natural movement. You placed the glass on my left palm while I kept the pull in my right hand, hidden. Only one finger, curled back, is necessary to hold it.

"Then, when I brought my hands together, I forced the cork into the glass. I gave a half-turn to the left, at the same time releasing the pull. The glass was whisked instantly out of sight beneath my coat. I pretended to rub the glass into nothingness—and there you are!"

"Gee, Jimmy, that's swell!" Tim exclaimed. "It's easy, too. I can do that one, can't I?"

"You can do them all, Tim, old-timer," Operator 5 answered, moving to the telephone. "A little practice, and you'll be able to fool everybody."

Tim inspected the pull intently as Jimmy Christopher stepped to the telephone and again called M-11. Z-7 answered.

Operator 5 spoke with firm decision. "We can gamble no more time on Bord, Chief. I am determined to make an attempt to draw out his memory. Please have these instructions followed carefully at the hospital while I'm on my way. All the furniture is to be removed from a room near Bord's. Assure him that he will soon be completely well, that he will be able to remember everything. It is important to impress that clearly on his mind. I am leaving at once!"

Jimmy Christopher jerked into his coat, pulled on his hat, and took up the box containing the strange motor device. Tim Donovan, quickly struggling into his mackinaw and cap, began to follow. "Jimmy—I'm coming with you!"

"Okay, old-timer. Dad, so long! Nan, I may have news for you soon."

"Good luck, son!" ex-Operator Q-6 exclaimed, seizing Operator 5's hand.

"And good luck from me, Jimmy," Diane said quietly as she went with him to the door.

THE HOSPITAL room was hushed. Bord sat alone in a chair beside a blinded window, staring blankly into space, his blunt fingers drumming. He had been allowed to dress; physically he was scarcely shaken, but the dullness of his eyes bespoke a clouded mind. He made no movement as he peered and blinked except the tapping of his fingers—until a nurse entered quietly.

She took his arm and he rose without protest. She led him along the silent corridor into another nearby room. Leaving him, she withdrew and shut the door. Bord looked curiously at the bare walls; his eyes came to rest upon a strange device on a small table.

It was like a small windmill with circular mirrors affixed to the arms. Upon it, a shaft of light played from a small spotlight affixed to the opposite wall. Bord tore his eyes from it and moved about; but again and again his gaze returned to the odd contrivance. Aimlessly he drifted—until a flutter of light filled the room, and he turned in mild surprise.

Slowly, the arms of the little windmill began revolving. The beam of light playing upon the mirrors sent reflections flashing into Bord's blank eyes. He began to turn away again, but his movement melted; he paused, peering at the sparkling mirrors as they revolved more rapidly, ever more rapidly....

He stood motionless, fascinated by the brilliance, the flash. He scarcely heard the sound when the door opened quietly. Operator 5 stepped silently into the room. He came without sound to Bord's side, bringing a stool with him. His voice droned as he said slowly: "Keep watching it, Bord. Keep watching it. You want to keep looking at it. Keep watching....

He sat the stool down, and at his touch, the spy sank to it. Bord stared steadily at the spinning vanes which were reflecting brilliant gleams into his eyes. A sigh came from his lungs as Operator 5 spoke in a hushed tone again.

"Watch the light. Never take your eyes from it. Keep watching it—watching it. The light hurts your eyes but you want to keep watching. You can't take your eyes from it because the brilliance draws them. Try, Bord—try to look away!"

The spy's head turned slowly, first to one side, then to the other—but his gaze remained fast on the spinning mirrors....

"You feel tired, Bord.... You want to rest.... Your eyes are smarting—you want to close them. Your eyelids are becoming heavier and heavier. You want to sleep—to sleep and rest. Close your eyes, Bord.... Close them.... Rest...."

The spy's lids dropped. He sighed again, deeply; his shoulders sagged. Operator 5, watching him intently, spoke in a voice that was itself sleepy and tired.

"You are resting now, and feeling better. Your head no longer aches. Your mind feels clearer. The clouds are melting away. Your brain is becoming sharper. You are beginning to remember now—to remember things you had forgotten. You can remember them if you wish. Try, Bord! Tell me your native country. Can you Remember?"

From Bord's lips came a sighing answer: "Yes!… Yes, I remember now!… I remember.… I am an Urakian.…"

"You are remembering now. You can remember anything you wish. Try, Bord I Try to remember what you were doing tonight. Try to recall what you said. You remember me—you remember my voice. Don't you, Bord?"

"I… remember.…"

OPERATOR 5 turned soundlessly, opened the door. Z-7 came in with a gliding step. Behind him, Tim Donovan tiptoed. They paused, peering at the flashing vanes of Operator 5's device, looking again at the man who sat with eyes closed.…

"You remember, Bord? You remember that you swore to tell me everything you know about the big gun. The big gun, Bord—it comes into your mind now. The name of Radi Havara—you remember that, Bord."

"Yes! Yes, I remember now!"

"The gun. Bord!" Operator 5 bent forward tensely. "Tell me! Where is it?"

"I—I do not know that."

Operator 5 glanced at Z-7. He whispered again to Bord:

"Radi Havara—she knows where the big gun is, Bord! You are sure of that!"

"Yes! Yes, she knows!"

"Where is she now, Bord? Where is she hiding? You swore to tell me!"

"I swore to tell…. I remember… yes! She—she is in a place high above the street…. The river flows by. It is… it is on a street… fifty. Yes—the river—the East River—the street is Fifti-eth…. The number…."

"Remember, Bord! Remember the number!"

"Six—yes, it is six—six—four—zero! I remember it now! Six—four—zero!… I am tired…."

Operator 5 straightened quickly, his eyes glittering with triumph. He saw Bord swaying upon the stool, heard the spy sigh profoundly. Again he pressed a whispered question.

"Is she there now, Bord? Is she?"

"No…. No, she is not there…. Her work demands that she move about…. She will not be there again until the next midnight."

Operator 5 took the man's arm. Bord rose, and they moved quietly to the door. Jimmy Christopher opened the way, directly droningly:

"You will go to your room now. You will sleep—sleep soundly. When you awake you will remember everything. You will be willing to tell us everything you know because you have sworn it. Go, Bord…. Go!"

The espionage agent walked with slow, shuffling steps to the door of his room. The nurse waiting there took his arm and escorted him inward. Operator 5 stood alert, his fingers straying to the death-charm on his watch-chain, until the door closed.

Z-7 blurted. "You have made him talk! All Dr. Hendricks could do was of no help, but you revived his memory! How?"

"Simple hypnosis, Chief," Jimmy Christopher answered quietly. "Suggestion, concentration, the induction of the hypnotic state. It brought from Bord's subconscious mind all that he had forgotten. This has been done many times before, but hypnotism is a force not in good standing with medical men."

CHAPTER 10
TIMED DOOM

ONE MINUTE of twelve, noon. Operator 5 sat tensely at his desk in Intelligence Headquarters M-11, New York, watching the spinning red second hand of the electric clock. Beside him, Z-7 sat silent. The secret suite was pervaded by a hush as the hour of doom approached.

Seconds whirred past. The red hand spun. The silence of the inner office persisted. Not until a full minute had passed did Z-7 move.

"No shell has struck near New York! If it had, we would surely have felt the shock!" He jerked up, and snapped open the door of the communications-room. He peered at the busy dispatchers, waiting. At last, grimly, he demanded: "Has report of a shell come in?"

"None, chief! All our headquarters are ready to flash the word the instant another hits—but no report has come in!"

Jimmy Christopher fingered reports on his desk. "It only means that the shell was not scheduled to fall at any point within the Eastern Standard time-zone. The shell that struck Chicago yesterday fell at twelve o'clock Central Standard Time. It means that the East is eliminated as the target of the big gun this time."

"Then we must wait for a report from somewhere in the Middle West! This damned waiting is driving me mad!"

Silently Operator 5 read a technical report submitted by Gustav Heist, the chemist on special service with the Intelligence. It was a complete analysis of the shell fragment found in Times Square. Jimmy Christopher rose, stepped to a filing-cabinet, and brought back a sheaf of papers of similar content. With the utmost care, he studied the data stating the percentages of carbon and silicon found in the steel of the burst shell.

He turned from this to charts prepared by radio experts in charge of the wireless directional-finders located along the Eastern seaboard. The direction of the Hertzian waves that had penetrated to the underground crypt were laid out, but the lines were almost parallel. Operator 5 flattened a map of the world, and quickly made computations. When he rose from his study, the hands of the electric clock were nearing the hour of one.

In the Central Standard time-zone, it was almost noon.

Again, with Z-7 at his side, he waited. The hush within the secret suite deepened. Minutes whirled past. The red second hand spun to the hour. Z-7 turned quickly, opened the door of the communications-room again. He waited, eyes smoldering—while the teletype receivers in the booths remained silent.

He demanded at last, impatiently: "No report? Are those wires open?"

"All wires check, Chief! There is no report!"

Jimmy Christopher turned darkened eyes upon Z-7. "The Central Time zone is eliminated, Chief. The shell may fall somewhere in the Mountain Time area."

"God! That's a vast territory—it's impossible to predict just where it will strike! It's the most diabolical attack ever planned!"

Jimmy Christopher agreed quietly. "Intricate calculations lie behind those shells, Chief. Even the time necessary for their flight from the muzzle of the big gun to the point of burst is computed!"

Z-7 BENT across the desk tensely. "It is impossible to exaggerate the state of terror that has seized our people. They are becoming crazed with fear. They are aroused to such a pitch of hysteria that anything may happen. The international situation is growing more acute every moment. The cry for war against England still rises; our government must soon yield, or the result may be a revolution."

"Chief," Operator 5 spoke ringingly, "I still say that the only hope lies in the destruction of that big gun. I am convinced that locating it is a far more gigantic task than we've dreamed. Without doubt, it is the hugest cannon ever built. Reaching it, destroying it, because of its range, may be next to impossible, but—"

He swiveled to the typewriter and tapped rapidly. When he turned back, holding a closely written form, he proffered it to Z-7.

"Ask the chief dispatcher to flash that message to every seismograph station in North and South America. I want them to send me their records of any earthquakes recorded just before each noon and each midnight the shells have fallen—all the data available. It's urgent!"

Z-7 passed the message to the communications-room and returned to peer at Operator 5 puzzledly. "What the devil have earthquake shocks got to do with the big gun?"

Operator 5 was already typing another order. He paused to answer: "That gun is so tremendous it must be anchored to bedrock. Its power is so great that its discharge may produce tremors through the earth's crust that seismographs can record exactly like a minor earthquake. There are so many small quakes every day taking place all over the world that we may not be able to isolate any recording of the big gun's discharges. It's a long gamble.

"But, if we can succeed in correlating data from all the seismographic stations, we will be able to determine the direction and the distance of those shocks. That will give us the location of the gun. And still—" Jimmy Christopher hesitated—"even knowing that location may help us very little. We may face such obstacles that we never can succeed in reaching it."

Z-7 blanched at the statement. He waited motionless until Operator 5 handed him further written orders.

"These orders are directing our sky-sounders, at all air fields, to listen into the sky at noon and midnight from now on. They will be able to pick up the sound of the coming shell before it is audible to the unaided ear. Included there are instructions for making reports as to direction, and for observing the Doppler effect.* The charts may help us to trace the trajectory of the shell—but again, it's a long chance."

Z-7 again passed the orders to the communications-room and returned to demand: "Why, in God's name, do you suggest that even if we locate the gun we may not be able to reach it?"

"That, Chief," Operator 5 answered slowly, "I dare not say until I have correlated this data. If what I suspect is true, we are literally finding ourselves in the very midst of the armed camp of Europe—with protective distances wiped out of existence!"

The second-hand of the electric clock spun its cycle of doom. Operator 5 busily examined reports and correlated them with data drawn from the inexhaustible files of the Intelligence archives. Slowly the hour passed—torturous tension mounted until again the minute-hand swung toward the hour mark....

Z-7 STOOD just inside the communications-room, waiting for word of the new destruction, hoping against hope that it would not come.... The teletypes were clicking, but the men

---

* AUTHOR'S NOTE: The Doppler effect is the change in the observed frequency of a vibration owing to the relative motion between the observer and the source of the vibration. In spectroscopy, this effect is a means of determining the motion of stars in the line of sight. The reader may have noticed, while traveling in a moving car past a ringing railway signal that the pitch of the sound heightens as the bell is approached and drops as it is left behind. The change in tone is only apparent, because of the relative motion of the listener to the sound-source.

attending them flipped their messages into routine baskets. The chief-dispatcher shook his head.

"Again no report!" Z-7 snapped, turning back to Jimmy Christopher. "There is only the Pacific time-zone left now! God, this waiting is worse than the news itself!"

"The whole country feels the same, Chief," Operator 5 declared quietly. "Radi Havara has planned to arouse terror to an uncontrollable pitch."

Z-7 paced across the office. "Somewhere on the Pacific Coast—but where? No man can know! At any vital point in that vast region! Somewhere on the Pacific Coast! God—it's unbearable!"

Jimmy Christopher peered at the clock. Z-7 watched it intently, haggardly. The Washington chief again paced the office as three o'clock neared—as noon approached on the Pacific Coast. Operator 5 rose quietly, and Z-7 came to a sharp stop, as the second hand reached its mark.

Jimmy Christopher strode into the communications-room. Z-7 pressed behind him. An uncanny silence filled the office usually humming and clattering. They stepped into the booth in which a teletype instrument sat, an open line connecting it with the Pacific Coast. Seconds ticked past while the machine remained inert.

Suddenly it sputtered into life. Operator 5 and Z-7 bent close, scarcely breathing. Out of the rollers twined a yellow tape carrying a message of doom:

... M-11 ... SHELL HEARD DESCENDING SHORTLY

BEFORE NOON PST ABOVE SAN FRANCISCO...
PLUNGED TO EARTH AT EMBARCADERO...
TERRIFIC CONCUSSION SHOOK ENTIRE CITY...
LARGE AREA DEVASTATED... TELEPHONIC
REPORTS NOW COMING STATE GREAT PIERS
DEMOLISHED... HUNDREDS DEAD AND THOU-
SANDS HURT... SHELL SWEPT TIDAL WAVE INTO
BAY... STEAMER STRUCK AND SINKING... TERROR-
IZED PEOPLE FLEEING SCENE... MILLIONS IN
PROPERTY DESTROYED... AMBULANCES AND
MILITIA CALLED... FLASH! ENEMY BOMB-
ERS HEADING TOWARD CITY FROM PACIFIC...
SQUADRON BLACK PLANES DRIVING TOWARD
HEART OF SAN FRANCISCO... OPERATOR A-2
REPORTS ARMY PLANES ORDERED UP AT CRISSY
FIELD... BOMBERS SWINGING DIRECTLY ABOVE
THE CITY....

The tape stopped, jerked out a broken sentence, stopped again.
Men crowded behind Operator 5 and Z-7, strained, haggard-
faced, waiting.... The clatter resumed in a burst:

... ARMY PLANES SWINGING TO ATTACK
BOMBERS... ATTACKING FORMATION FLYING
ABOVE PRESIDIO... BOMBS STRIKE TELEGRAPH
HILL... ANTI-AIRCRAFT BATTERIES BELCH AT
ATTACKING PLANES... CRISSY FIELD CRATES
HITTING ATTACKERS... A-2 REPORTS SQUAD-
RON COMMANDER DECLARES NO MEN IN

PITS OF PLANES... ROBOT SHIPS FLOWN BY
RADIO CONTROL... ARMY FLYERS SEEKING
CONTROLLING SHIPS... BOMBS CONTINUE TO
DROP... MARKET STREET HIT....

"Manless planes!" Z-7 blurted.
Still the teletype chattered its report.

... CRISSY REPORTS ONE RADIO-CONTROL
PLANE SHOT DOWN... OTHER DRIVEN TO SEA...
ROBOT BOMBERS FALLING... TWO CRASHED IN
GOLDEN GATE... A-2 REPORTS ARMY SQUAD-
RON COMMANDER HAS SIGHTED CAMOU-
FLAGED AIRPLANE CARRIER AT SEA... CRISSY
SHIPS SWARMING TO ATTACK... ROBOT ATTACK
REPULSED BY QUICK ACTION AND WARNING OF
GENERAL STAFF TO STAND READY... SECOND
CONTROL SHIP DOWN... AIRPLANE CARRIER
FIRED UPON... DISGUISED SHIP HIT BY EXPLO-
SION... DANGER OF BOMBERS ENDED BUT CITY
STUNNED BY VICIOUS SWIFTNESS OF ATTACK....

CHAPTER 11
MIDNIGHT DISAPPEARANCE

THICK, FEATHERY snow swirled from murky darkness to whiten afresh the spires and chasms of New York.
Lights gleamed hazily through the wafting veil. Sounds were

deadened. All the city lay hushed and fearful amid the beauty of the storm as midnight neared....

Quiet lay deep over the piers and the empty dead-end streets flanking the East River. Cranes reared like long-necked ghosts in the gloom. Tugs chuffed over the inky water with lights twinkling dimly through the beating snow. Far away, foghorns hooted their dismal warnings. Waves lapped coldly under the span of the Queensboro Bridge. Over all the murky scene lay a hushed tension.

In a bleak doorway, coat-collars turned high against the flying flakes, unseen in the veiled shadows, Operator 5, Z-7 and Tim Donovan stood eyeing a building on the opposite side of the street. Its windows shown faintly with the glow of night-lights burning in the vast rooms beyond. It was a distributing point of a nationally known manufacturer—its address was that whispered by the espionage agent Bord when hypnotized.

Midnight crept closer....

The entrance of the huge building was brightly lighted, but during the past half hour no one had passed through it. Jimmy Christopher waited motionless until a vague, shuffling figure came into the shafting light revealed as a stooped woman, a ragged shawl drawn tightly over her head. White hair fluffed as she bent against the river wind. Beneath her bulky skirts broken shoes covered her feet. She shambled pitifully into the entrance and the door closed behind her.

Operator 5 stepped into the street. Z-7 and Tim Donovan were about to follow when he paused abruptly, and signaled them back quickly.

Along the sidewalk another figure was approaching. This was a young man, erect, hat pulled low against the flurry, his strides long and swift. He shoved through the entrance of the warehouse and vanished. Jimmy Christopher drifted away again.

He shifted, with Z-7 and Tim Donovan at his side, so that he could see beyond the frosted panes of the swinging doors. In the foyer, the old woman had opened a closet. She was shaking off her shawl, lifting out a mop and pail. The young man strode past her into the open cage of an elevator. It whirred upward as the old woman filled her pail at the closet sink. Carrying it, clutching a cake of soap in one quaking hand, she shambled to the grille and waited until the elevator cab reappeared.

It whisked upward with her as Operator 5 strode to the entrance. He glanced at his watch, saw that it lacked only a few minutes of midnight. Z-7 and Tim Donovan followed him to the elevator grille. There they waited, Jimmy Christopher's eyes shone dark.

Inside the shaft, the cable whirred; with a click, the grille slid open. Operator 5 stepped in, glancing warily at the gorilla of a man at the control. Z-7 and Tim Donovan followed as the big man glared: "Where do you think you're going?"

Operator 5 said: "All the way up."

"I don't know you," the attendant countered gruffly. "I ain't allowed to take anybody up after hours unless—"

OPERATOR 5'S answer was to slide the grille shut. He faced the attendant squarely, commanded again: "Up!"

"It's against the rules," the attendant mumbled, apparently cowed, as he thrust at the control.

The car whirred upward. Floor-levels flashed past as Jimmy Christopher stood silent. When the car bounded to a stop, the big man slid the grille open to disclose a vast space beyond, partitioned into offices. They were empty and lightless save for the gleam of a few scattered globes.

"Well?" the attendant demanded as Operator 5 stood unmoving.

"I said," he answered quietly, *"all* the way up! Drop your hand!"

The fingers of the attendant had risen to his vest and gripped what appeared to be an ordinary fountain-pen. At Jimmy Christopher's sharp command, he flicked it out and leveled it like a gun. A sharp click sounded as Operator 5 snatched at it. Instantly, greenish fumes spurted onto the air.

Jimmy Christopher dropped to a swift crouch beneath the gusting vapor. He gripped the big man's arms and swung. Z-7 gave a choking sob; Tim Donovan shoved toward the door. Operator 5 propelled the attendant through the open grille, into the gloomy office beyond. Behind him, the Washington chief followed, gasping, as Tim Donovan bounded into clearer air.

The big attendant snarled with fury as Operator 5 forced him out of the cab. He struck a vicious blow that slid off Jimmy Christopher's shoulder. Fumes clouded into the partitioned space as Operator 5 sprang aside, and struck out. His stiffened fingers drove to the side of the big man's neck. The attendant moaned, sagged to his knees.

Jimmy Christopher bent over him as he rolled flat, quickly felt his pulse, and straightened.

"Stay away from that gas!" he warned. "It's Green Cross—

trichlormethylchloroformate! It will eat into your lungs and drown you in your own blood if you get enough of it!"

Z-7 was gasping for air; stinging tears were gathering in Tim Donovan's eyes. "He exploded a cartridge of Green Cross in a fountain-pen gun," Jimmy Christopher declared tightly. "He thought he'd imprison us in that cab while he slipped out. Stay back until it's gone!"

At Operator 5's side, Tim Donovan and Z-7 waited silently while the mist melted away in the air. The offices were silent. When they stepped forward alertly, into the cab, pressing handkerchiefs over their noses, Jimmy Christopher threw the control handle, sent the cab whirring upward again. At the next level he stopped it. He slipped his automatic into his band and stood at the door listening.

Slowly, silently, he eased the sliding panels aside. A small, dark room, three doors in its walls, each closed lay beyond. Jimmy Christopher stooped, whisked aside the Persian rug which spread across the floor. He pointed at a series of small, copper circles set into the wood and straightened, smiling tightly.

"Don't step on them! They're electric contacts. They'll ring alarms in the rooms beyond."

QUICKLY HE opened one door, found it to be an empty closet. The second was also a closet. Operator 5 drew on a glove before he touched the knob of the third. He tried it, found it locked. He brought his pack of master-keys from his pocket, inserted one into the keyhole.

Leaning close to the panels, as he worked, he heard vague

voices beyond. A woman's said: "You are on time. You have the letter?"

Operator 5's eyes narrowed as he felt the bolt draw back. He signaled to Z-7 and Tim Donovan, straightened, turning the knob, tensing....

Suddenly a hoarse exclamation sounded, blending into a woman's startled cry. At the far end of the spacious, richly decorated room, the pair whirled away from the table at which they were standing. One was the young man who had entered the building only a moment ago. The other was the disheveled cleaning-woman. As she turned her face full toward Operator 5, the light glinted upon her hair—hair not white now, but youthfully blonde. The bright eyes that flashed defiance at Jimmy Christopher were the eyes of Radi Havara!

Both persons whirled through an open doorway behind them as Operator 5 bounded forward. The door flashed shut as he shouted a forbidding command. He sprang to face it, snapped over his shoulder to Z-7 and Tim Donovan: "Find a way out! Get onto the roof!"

He heard their quick, answering movements as he gripped the knob. Inside the room beyond, a gun blasted. The bullet splintered the panel beside Operator 5's head as he thrust in. He sprang aside, swinging his automatic to answer the shot. A flash of bright flame from a table stopped him short.

One window of the room was flung wide, and snow was swirling in. Beside it, at the table, the young man was backing away. On an ashtray, a crumpled sheet of paper, just ignited, was flaring. Jimmy Christopher sprang forward again as the gun in the espionage agent's hand roared.

Spattering lead struck Operator 5's automatic, tore it from his fingers. Stunned with sudden pain, he reached with his left for the flaming paper. He snatched it up and crushed it into his palm. The blaze seared his skin even as it snuffed out Jimmy Christopher's movement was a continuous whirl that brought him to face the espionage agent as gunmetal flashed again.

His numbed right hand darted to his belt, clicked loose the clasp. A shot crashed and a bullet ripped through the sleeve of his coat as he whisked out the long, narrow sheath covering a rapier of Toledo steel. Jimmy Christopher whipped the supple blade at the spy's gun as it turned upon him again.

Steel clashed steel. Magical power played along the hissing *épée*. The sharp edge slashed the hand gripping the gun and the spy cried out in sudden agony. The stinging point paralyzed his forefinger even as it bore again on the trigger. Uncannily, the blade seized the weapon, snatched it away. Jimmy Christopher whisked it against the chest of the spy.

"Back up!"

Mad fury blazed in the espionage agent's eyes as he lunged forward. Operator 5 made no move; but a tremor passed through the rapier. The spy twisted back again, in agonized astonishment, peering down at the cut in his shirt that seeped deep red. He spun about, clutching the deep wound—dropped.

Jimmy Christopher lowered the crimson blade. "If you had obeyed—!"

The crash of a shot sounded beyond. He whirled back into

the sumptuous studio, saw a door flung wide and snow gusting in on the wind. Z-7 staggered into the light, gun-arm dropping, left hand clutched around it while the fingers trickled blood. He straightened in agony against the jamb, gasped: "She's gone—into that!"

Operator 5 sprang into the darkness of a flat, open roof. He saw no movement until he was halfway toward a huge super-structure at the corner—the water-tank of a fire-system. In the snow, a small figure was squirming. Jimmy Christopher crouched beside Jim Donovan.

The boy was sobbing, trying to rise, stunned by a vicious blow that had marked a ghastly welt across his face. He yelled, "She went in there—in there! She—!"

OPERATOR 5 hurried toward the huge cylindrical tank. Its base sat flush upon the roof; unlike most water-tanks it had no conical roof, and no iron bands circled it Jimmy Christopher, as he moved toward it, heard a sharp hissing. He groped along the curving wall, felt the edge of a door cut into the wood. He shouldered against it, found it bolted. A quick, rustling sound came from inside as he whirled back.

Swiftly, a huge black shadow rose from the interior of the tank—shot upward at lightning speed into the swirling air. In the flash of a second, it whisked high above—a dead-black balloon, fatly inflated. In a harness fastened to the tight shrouds,

Swiftly a huge black shadow arose from the interior of
the tank—shot upward at lightning speed!

a figure dangled—a woman! Her skirts tore in the wind as the bag flew upward through the night....

Operator 5's automatic blazed three times. He did not shoot at the swinging figure, but toward the balloon. Its ascent was so swift that it had vanished before the first pull of the trigger. In the thick darkness above, wind-currents were whirling the falling snow—whisking the balloon away. Again Operator 5 fired, twice, and waited. The snow flaked down through air into which the balloon had flashingly vanished....

Operator 5 snapped over his shoulder: "Call headquarters, Chief! Have the police radio cars signaled! Order them to watch the city at all points. That balloon has got to come down somewhere and Radi Havara with it!"

Z-7 hurried into the penthouse to speed the alarm. Operator 5 thrust again at the closed door of the tank. He hurled his weight against it three times as the screws holding the bolts gave. He stumbled into the cylindrical hollow space, open at the top. Lined along the walls were compressed-gas tanks. Hanging on nails were several hooks such as had carried J-4's body into the night sky. Neatly folded at one side lay other silken balloons, deflated. The apparatus confirmed only too plainly Operator 5's explanation of Radi Havara's means of disposing of the dead bodies of Intelligence agents—how she had escaped tonight....

Jimmy Christopher hurried out as Tim Donovan came swaying to his side. The boy was dazed by the blow that had downed him. Grimly he kept at Operator 5's side as they entered the modernistic room. At a telephone, Z-7, was standing, his face white, his sleeve dripping blood.

"Yes! Good God! Yes! Find that woman! Do everything humanly possible to find that woman!…"

He thumped the instrument down, stared haggardly at Jimmy Christopher.

"Another shell has fallen! It plunged into Boston Common at exactly midnight! The State House has been damaged and hundreds of people struck down in the streets! The details are coming into M-11 now!"

Operator 5's eyes clouded dark as he stepped into the adjoining room. He closed the door upon the still form of the espionage agent. He opened his palm, gazed grimly at the crumpled, charred paper he still held. Carefully, at the desk, he unfolded it. Across its broken surface, cryptic words were scrawled.

"Chief," Operator 5 said briskly, "our chance of learning the location of the big gun from Radi Havara is gone—unless this communication carries that information. It's possible that that young man had just reported to Radi Havara for duty and his instructions may be connected somehow with the cannon. This must be deciphered as soon as possible!"

"You're the man to do it, Operator 5!" Z-7 exclaimed. "I'll order several agents from M-11 to guard the place. We must search it for possible evidence—but in the meantime you can try to solve that cipher. If that message gives the location of the big gun—pray God we will be able to translate it before the next twelve o'clock comes!"

Operator 5 nodded tensely. He placed the ragged sheet carefully in an envelope, retrieved his gun and replaced his rapier. He strode rapidly to the entrance of Radi Havara's hidden headquarters. His fingers strayed unconsciously to the golden skull glittering on his watch-chain.

UNDER A bright, low-hanging light, sitting tensely at his desk in the inner office at M-11, Operator 5 studied the mysterious symbols of the cipher message.

With Z-7 and Tim Donovan, he had returned immediately to the secret Intelligence headquarters. The Washington chief's wounded arm had been bound. The bruise across Tim Donovan's face had been treated. They both watched intently as Operator 5 strove to pierce the secret of the cryptogram.

"One of the most difficult ciphers known, Chief," he remarked quietly. "It is not included in the Urakian code-book. It makes me feel all the more that this message is vastly important. Still—"

He wrote rapidly as he broke off. Again there was silence in the office. Each passing moment tightened Z-7's nerves. He whirled when the communications-room opened and the chief-dispatcher strode in with a flimsy.

"Report from C-23. He states that he believes Radi Havara dropped from the balloon in a parachute. He is not certain, but an abandoned 'chute has just been found on a pier near Wall street. It is known that a motor-boat put out from that point a short time ago. The Harbor Patrol is on the job. The East River is being searched, but if Radi Havara has taken to a boat, finding her is almost impossible in this storm!"

Operator 5 worked steadily at the message after the dispatcher returned to his desk while Z-7 strode the office. Almost another hour passed when the telephone jangled and the Washington chief snatched it up.

"H-14 reporting from the hospital. Following your orders, I have been questioning Bord. There is absolutely no more information to be obtained from him, though his memory is functioning clearly now. He doesn't know where the big gun is located."

In the communications-room, a teletype was clattering. Z-7's jaw-muscles bunched as he read the message brought him by the chief-dispatcher. Grimly he exclaimed: "The international situation is growing more dangerous every hour! Washington has just relayed dispatches received from Tokyo and Mukden. Open statements have been made there that in case of war, the United States will ally herself with Russia! Reports made earlier in the summer were only hints*—these are outspoken! Japan and Great Britain against the United States and Russia! The whole world is threatened by the dynamite of these reports—the cunning work of Radi Havara!"

Again the communications-room snapped open; again the chief-dispatcher brought a report to the pallid-faced Z-7.

"Another report concerning Radi Havara, from L-8 at Roos-

---

* AUTHOR'S NOTE: Z-7 is referring to cable dispatches distributed by the Associated Press under the dates of August 16 and 17 last summer. In part, these reports read:

"TOKYO, Friday, Aug. 17—The Japanese press was publishing today threats of military action against the Soviet as a result of another dangerous situation in Manchuria. Negotiations over the disposition of the Chinese Eastern Railway are deadlocked. According to a dispatch to the Asahi, Japanese army leaders in Manchukuo believe the Russians plotted to disrupt the rail-

evelt Field! He declares that a plane has just taken off, carrying a woman, and the woman is believed to be Radi Havara! She climbed into it at the last moment, before she could be stopped, and the plane flew north. It is a mysterious craft which has been kept locked and under guard in a special hangar. Rumors say it was built for a secret long flight and that it carries a vast store of fuel. There's no further report on it, Chief!"

"If Radi Havara is in that plane, it means that she will escape the country! You've forced her to that, Operator 5!"

"Or else," Jimmy Christopher said quietly, "her work is done, Chief! Nothing remains save the outbreak of a war that will wipe us out of existence—a war that will ravage this hemisphere and leave Urakia untouched!"

AGAIN HE worked a long time intently. Abruptly he straightened, and his pencil flew. When he rose, he was holding a closely-written sheet in his hand, and his eyes were shin-

way's service in order... to test the extent to which disruption would hamper Japan's military movements in the event of conflict."

"MUKDEN, Manchukuo, Aug. 16.—M. Kuznetsoff, Russian vice-president of the Chinese Eastern Railway, is purported to have made a speech today which is highly potent in its scarcely veiled intimations. He said in part:

" 'The world powers understand the danger of Japanese armaments. Therefore in the crisis of 1935-36, if Japan wants to disturb the peace, a third country will assist us.' "

The whole world buzzed with the question: Did this "third country" mean the United States?

ing dark. "There it is, Chief!" he said proffering the paper. Z-7 rapidly read the astounding translation:

> RH—This credential introduces our agent X-10. He is a highly skilled artilleryman and he is to assume duty at once at the big gun. You must provide for his safe journey to its location for no one else can do so. Since not even you know its location, it is necessary for me to give you this information. The cannon is located on a lofty plateau in the Rocky Mountains, east of the Continental Divide and 40 air miles north-west-by-west from Denver, Colorado. X-10 must approach it alone and—

The Washington chief broke off, his black eyes smoldering with grim triumph.

"At last we know! Its location is certainly guarded, but it can be reached easily by air! We will be able to destroy it with bombs! There is scarcely time to reach it before it will fire the next shell!"

Operator 5 gazed intently at Z-7. "Chief, knowing the character of Radi Havara, I—"

"But you've found it! We must not waste a moment!" Z-7 whirled to the chief-dispatcher, snapped: "Get General MacBride on the wire at once!"

Jimmy Christopher spoke no word as the Washington chief waited anxiously for the connection to go through. When the bell jangled he snatched up the telephone. Breathlessly he declared: "General MacBride, we have located the big gun! It is hidden on a plateau in the Rockies, forty miles from Denver! Operator 5 discovered the secret and I suggest that he lead an attack of bombers upon it. Flash Mitchell Field at once and order two of the fastest ships to be prepared for us. At the same time, signal Brooks Field, Texas, to hold a flight of bombers ready and to wait for wireless orders so that it will reach the objective with Operator 5. Speed is absolutely necessary if we wish to reach that gun before it fires the next shell!"

Z-7 turned from the telephone to declare: "MacBride is sending out those orders now! We must leave for Mitchell Field at once!"

Jimmy Christopher's lips tightened wryly. "You are convinced, Chief, that this is the move to make?"

"You are the man to lead that flight, yes!"

"I will follow your orders. Yet, I believe—" His voice faded. He peered again at the charts on his desk. He raised to Z-7's face eyes that had turned from blue to deep black.

"Chief, this move, like every other we have made, is a great gamble—but there is nothing else we can do. We'll leave for Mitchell Field at once. Yet I'm convinced, Chief, that regardless of what we accomplish with the bombers—even though we destroy that big gun hidden in the Rockies—another shell will fall at the scheduled time—noon!"

He stroke briskly to the door while Z-7 stared after him in utter, dismayed bewilderment....

CHAPTER 12
BIG GUN BELOW!

ACROSS TERRITORY blanketed with snow, roaring at a swift speed with sunlight glistening on their wings, two U.S. Army pursuits drove westward—toward a remote plateau in the Rockies.

Wing to wing they sped over whitened cities and villages, over ribboning roads, across ice-flaked rivers. The ace pilots in their pits coaxed the utmost power from the motors in a straining race against time. The sun flew westward with them and an invisible thread of radio bound them to the earth.

In one, Operator 5 listened to reports flashing through the short-wave radio equipment, and periodically he returned news of his progress. In the other, Z-7 heard the same voice speaking from secret Intelligence Headquarters WDC-13 in Washington, the center of all undercover activities of the government. Both were helmeted, goggled, bundled in coveralls lined with sheepskin against the bitter cold of the wind.

"Calling Three-two!" the voice from Washington sang. "It is just past high noon in the Eastern Standard Time belt No report of another shell has been received."

Steadily the planes droned westward. Operator 5 heard and gave wireless reports. The flashing wings traced their way across the cold sky at top speed while an hour passed. Again a report flashed from WDC-13:

"It is now noon in the Central Time zone! Again there is no report of a shell falling. Another hour will tell whether or not the gun is trained this time on any spot within the Mountain Time division!"

And still the two planes flashed their path across the sky, driving at terrific speed toward their objective. They were special crates with fuel capacity great enough to fly the whole distance without the necessity of landing. The engines functioned to perfection while terrain that began to grow rugged unrolled beneath them.

"We are entering the Mountain time-belt!" Operator 5 reported over the ether. "At our present speed, we will be able to reach our objective before noon."

"Major Henley, commanding the bombing flight from Brooks Field, has flashed a report," the voice replied. "He has timed the hop perfectly. Before long you will catch sight of his formation."

Time passed swiftly as the pursuits struck across rising foot-hills. Far in the distance, the looming humps of the mountains appeared on the horizon. Minute by minute, their masses expanded, disclosing snow-capped peaks, vast stony ranges. Towns moved past, deep in drifted snow. Operator 5 searched the sky through binoculars.

At last he glimpsed black moving specks in the distance. A smart V formation of planes was moving in a course diagonal to his. He reported briskly: "The bombers are in sight!"

He trimmed the radio-transmitter, spoke into the microphone suspended before his lips: "Calling Major Henley!"

Out of the air the answer came: "At your service!"

"We are approaching! Swing your formation to follow us as we pass Denver!"

OUT OF the sky the roaring bombers flashed closer. Magnificent Martin monoplanes, capable of a speed that could elude lighter pursuits in war-time maneuvers, they glistened brightly in the sun. Beneath them, the mountain-peaks glittered, snow-wreathed, a scene of breathtaking beauty—a hazard of tremendous danger. The Martins swung slowly as the city of Denver neared; the V moved to follow the planes carrying Operator 5 and Z-7.

Jimmy Christopher noted that the electric clock on the dash was indicating less than half an hour before noon, Standard Mountain Time. Denver passed below.

Operator 5 spoke orders to his pilot. The plane shifted to a course calculated to carry it directly above the lofty plateau mentioned in the cipher message. Due northwest by west the Martins followed. As the distance melted, Jimmy Christopher peered overside, searching the vast depths and heights of the range. Beyond loomed the crest of the Rockies, the great Continental Divide which was the watershed of a nation.

Faintly, in the vast billowing spread of white, he discerned a darker spot "Lower!" he ordered his pilot.

The plane howled downward while Z-7's flew alongside it. The decreasing altitude enlarged the black area in the vast spread of snow. Through his binoculars Jimmy Christopher peered.

"Calling Major Henley!" he sang into the microphone. "Directly below us, evergreens are apparently growing far above the timber line. It is a camouflage. Bombers ready!"

Then, out of the dark mass, a streak of light appeared—the sun reflecting off shining metal. Gun below!

Operator 5 called into the air: "Major Henley! Note my position! Our objective is directly beneath me! The dark spot is camouflage, covering a gun location. The crew is observing us. There may be anti-aircraft batteries below ready to protect the cannon. Swing into position as rapidly as possible and report when you are ready!"

"Yes, sir!"

Operator 5 commanded his pilot: "Up!" Through his powerful glasses, as the plane soared with Z-7's tracing its course, he saw men running across the plateau. The shelf had been cleared of snow and layered with evergreen branches. The outlines of the gun were not discernible through them, except for an occasional glint of the sun upon the barrel. Swiftly, as Operator 5 spiraled up, the bombers dived directly at their mark.

"Major Henley calling! We are ready!"

Instantly Operator 5 ordered: "Bombs!"

From the racks of the flashing Martins, sleek projectiles dropped. Glinting, spinning, shrieking, vaned bombs streaked down, released in pairs as the Martins howled, one after another, above their mark. Through his glasses, Jimmy Christopher watched the spinning projectiles streak—closer and closer to the isolated plateau!

They struck! Flame blossomed among the white. Gushing smoke sprang into the rarefied air. Rumbling explosions echoed high into the sky to penetrate the roar of the motors. With uncanny accuracy the bombs flashed down to unleash their power.

Into the midst of the holocaust, Operator 5 peered through the binoculars. He saw the huge, black barrel of the cannon shift. Snow clouded from the shelf, exposing bleak rock. Through a haze of vapor, the terrific destruction of the exploding bombs became plainly evident. Operator 5 spoke ringingly again into the spider microphone.

"Calling Major Henley! Cease bombing! The gun is down!"

Operator 5 trimmed his transmitter and called: "Chief! I'm going to land!"

He issued orders to his pilot. Immediately, the pursuit began a swift spiral downward, while Z-7's crate circled above and the bevy of bombers swung wide. The crate swooped low above the plateau. Operator 5 saw at close range the terrific destruction brought by the bombs. In the midst of bared and broken rock he perceived a long-barreled cannon lying on its side—a barrel that appeared to have been broken. Eyes narrowed, he continued to peer at the amazing sight while his pilot sent the pursuit mushing down….

IT SETTLED into an area of ragged white, surrounded by rearing spires, deserted and silent save for the droning of the engines in the sky. The trucks of the pursuit jounced upon an irregular rock surface. Brakes cramped hard against the wheels. Halfway across the shelf, the pursuit stopped.

Operator 5 paused only to peer at the clock on the dash. Its hands indicated less than two minutes of twelve, Mountain Time. He legged over the cowling, ran toward the site of the big gun. About it sprawled the broken bodies of men who had attended it; the massive piece lay banked in upthrown snow. His eyes grew dark when he saw that the great barrel had snapped like a twig.

As he hurried back to the plane, his pilot exclaimed: "It's not possible that the bombs could have broken the gun like that!"

"Not possible—but it was done!" Operator 5 climbed into the pit of his plane, shifted the tuning condensers to the wavelength of Z-7's wireless equipment.

"Chief, I thought so! The gun was brought here in segments—even the barrel. The barrel has been held together by thin bands of steel. One shell fired in it would have burst it to pieces. It means that—"

Z-7 blurted: "What the devil! You mean to say—?"

"Chief! Listen!"

"Good God—I hear it! *Another shell—coming now!*"

Operator 5 peered into the bright sky, nerves tense, lips pressed tight. Through the mountain air a cry was sounding—a shrill, sharp wail that grew louder each second! It was the banshee shriek of a projectile flying through its trajectory—a shell flying somewhere overhead! As the note rose in pitch, as its volume swelled, the ominous streak of light appeared across the heavens—the trail of descending doom! For a long, tense minute the scream continued. Then, from the distance, thunder rumbled. The shell had struck!

Through the ear-'phones pressed to Operator 5's ears the voice of Z-7 rasped: "It has hit Denver! Good God—from this position it seems to have plunged into the very center of the city! I saw the flash clearly—smoke is clouding up now! In God's name—!"

Operator 5 waited to hear no more. He trimmed his transmitter grimly. Sharply he called: "WDC-13! Operator 5 signaling WDC-13!"

"Go ahead!"

"We have succeeded in destroying the gun located here, but another shell had just fallen—into Denver! Direct the bombers back to their base! I will fly to Washington as fast as my plane can get me there. In the meantime, there are important instructions to be followed. Waste no time about them!"

"What! You say—"

"Listen! The government has acquired a Sikorsky S-42, specially reconstructed, and it is hangared on Boiling Field. I want that ship made ready for a long flight as soon as possible!" *

"Yes, sir!"

"Part of its payload capacity is to be utilized for reserve fuel tanks so that the ship can fly 4,000 miles non-stop. At the same time, the following are to be prepared and put aboard it:

* AUTHOR'S NOTE: S-42 is the designation of a giant airplane designed and built by the famed Igor Ivan Sikorsky. On its final test flight for Pan-American Airways, it broke eight world's records by flying the greatest load the greatest distance at the greatest speed. The ship has a gross weight of 19 tons and a top speed of 192 miles per hour. The first of these ships to go into service, between North and South America, was christened the *Brazilian Clipper* by the wife of President Vargas of Brazil. Sikorsky designed the great craft in accordance with specifications outlined by Colonel Charles Lindbergh, who accompanied it on its final trial flight. It is the forerunner of a regular trans-oceanic mail and messenger service. The S-42 is, however, strictly a flying boat. Its retractable trucks are used only when wheeling it in and out of the water. The specially reconstructed S-42 mentioned here by Operator 5 is one altered so that it can take-off and land on the ground, as well as the water, with equal ease.

Two army observation balloons; sufficient compressed helium to inflate these balloons each twice; one hundredweight of quick-setting cement; two hundred and fifty feet of rubber hosing two inches in diameter. Order built up at once a block of balsa wood four inches thick and four feet square.* Other orders will follow while I fly to Washington—but these are absolutely essential, and no time must be lost in providing them!"

Jimmy Christopher twisted the dials back to Z-7's wavelength.

"Chief, we're returning to the East now—to Washington, at top speed!" From the plane circling over the plateau, Z-7 peered down. He saw Operator 5's plane crawl across the bare rock; he saw it launch into the air. It spiraled up, and he ordered his pilot to follow. Swiftly it leveled and, with its motor thundering at the limit of its power, streaked across mountains and sky....

INTELLIGENCE HEADQUARTERS WDC-13 was hidden so carefully behind the drab store-fronts of one of the radiating avenues of Washington, D.C., that lifelong residents of the capital might never suspect its existence. Into this window-less series of rooms, Operator 5 and Z-7 codeworded their way after a waiting car had carried them swiftly from Boiling Field, immediately upon their landing.

---

* AUTHOR'S NOTE: Balsa wood, the pith of a South American tree, weighs only seven or eight pounds a cubic foot and is the lightest wood known. Since it is not obtainable in larger pieces than about six inches thick and eight or nine feet long, it is cut and glued together in order to make sections of different sizes.

Striding to Z-7's desk, Operator 5 immediately called the chief dispatcher from the communications-room. "I ordered certain reports brought from New York."

"They're here, sir!" The dispatcher drew a folder from a file cabinet placed it in Operator 5's hands. "I have word that your plane will be ready soon. Your later orders, given during your flight back, are being carried out."

Z-7 peered at Jimmy Christopher haggardly as he spread the reports on the table, and brought large-scale maps from another cabinet.

"I am completely at a loss, Operator 5! You have had no opportunity to explain matters to me—"

"That gun, Chief," Operator 5 declared quietly, "is somewhere in Europe!"

Z-7 stared. "God—is it possible?"

"I'm obliged to remind you, Chief, that when the first news of the German's 'Big Bertha' was brought to the British Intelligence by 'The Dane' he was not believed." *

---

* AUTHOR'S NOTE: The spy known as "The Dane" during the World War was a maritime engineer traveling in Germany. Captain Henry Landau, Chief in the Field of the British Secret Service with headquarters then in Holland, has termed him the greatest of the Allied war-time spies. He possessed a prodigious memory and was able to carry in his head countless complex specifications of war-engines being built by the Germans. It was he who first reported the existence of "Big Bertha" and, as Operator 5 declares, he was not believed. He is now living in his native village where he is an honored and wealthy citizen.

"True, but—"

"All the evidence points to it, Chief! First, the fact that no gun-reports were heard anywhere in the United States. Second, the fact that Gustav Heist's analysis shows that the steel of the shells is different in composition from any forged in this country. Since such shells could not be brought across our borders unnoticed, it means that they were fired from abroad. This seismographic data I expect to verify that. You understand now, Chief, what I meant when I said that we are finding ourselves in the midst of the armed camp of Europe. That gun has wiped away the protection of three thousand miles of ocean!"

"Yes! I understand! Then Radi Havara—"

"Duped us again. I suspected it at once, but it was that way. She knew, because Bord had been captured, that we would seek her out. She staged that scene in her penthouse last night in order to trick us. That secret message was faked—she meant us to be deluded by its false information—a play for more time. Each hour brings the international crisis nearer, and she is well aware of it!"

"She tricked me completely!"

"We must make up for that lost time, Chief! The location of that gun must be found as soon as possible. The indications are that the explosive used in it is superite, and that in itself is of no help since most nations are using superite or TNT for their big guns now.* I suspect, Chief, that our sky-sounders will be

---

* AUTHOR'S NOTE: When first high explosive was used in projectiles, each nation used a type peculiar to itself. The French used *Melinite*, the Germans

able to tell us nothing. Everything depends upon these seismographic records."

OPERATOR 5 quickly examined the data which had been sent by wireless and cable in response to his requests from stations at scattered points in North and South America. He worked with slide-rule, made complex computations, charted lines on a map of the world. For the better part of an hour, he worked intently while Z-7 watched anxiously. When he straightened, he pointed to converging lines he had drawn on the map—lines which crossed at a point in Central Europe. "That gun, Chief, is in Urakia!"

"Great God! That is what you meant when you said that insurmountable obstacles might keep us from reaching it!"

"Yes. The hugest gun ever conceived and built. It's range is possible because the projectiles rise far above the troposphere, to the very limits of the stratosphere, where no air resistance retards their flight. The calculated cunning behind those shells is appalling. The master of that gun must take into consideration the temperature, the barometric pressure, the degree of wear on the barrel, the factor of sea-level, and even the revolution of the earth during the time of flight—but by the aid of radio control, the projectile is able to come down with unwavering accuracy on its point of burst. I repeat, Chief, we cannot save ourselves from annihilation now except by the destruction of that gun."

"But in God's name, how—?"

Granatfullung 88, the British *Lyddite* and the Japanese *Shimose*. Later propellants are *Cordite, Röhrenpulver, N.C.T., Ballisite,* and *Flake.*

"We must wireless immediately our four agents in Urakia. Instruct them to investigate this suspicious area south of Urol, the capital of Urakia, where the big gun is apparently located. Tell them that I will communicate with them at their headquarters by wireless. The blow to destroy that gun must be struck carefully."

Z-7 demanded quickly: "You're going to attempt to reach that gun?"

"I am. I have ordered a plane made ready—our S-42. The crew is waiting. It means, Chief, a non-stop flight across the Atlantic to a position near that gun and—"

Z-7 peered wide-eyed. "That is almost certain suicide! This is the worse possible time of year for such a flight so far as weather is concerned. Even if you succeed in reaching Urakia, you will then have placed yourself in the position of a spy in a foreign country. That means, if you are caught—death! We will be able to do nothing to help you because an apprehended secret-agent must be repudiated by his own government!"

"True, Chief. But I cannot let that hold me back. I plan to take off here as soon as possible, so as to reach Urakia—if I reach it at all—at night. Speed is essential because, during the flight of the S-42, more shells will fly from that gun into this country—the international situation will reach a crisis. No time must be lost!"

Z-7's face turned white. "To reach Urakia by the shortest route, you will be obliged to fly across Germany. That in itself is a serious danger. I need not remind you of the ghastly rumors concerning the Lithuanian flyers Darius and Girenas."*

"It is a task, Chief," Jimmy Christopher answered, "which I

---

* AUTHOR'S NOTE: The rumors to which Z-7 is referring here have not been voiced by the press in the United States, though they are of startling character and of international significance. On July 15, 1933, at 5:24 a.m., Captain Stephen Darius and Lieutenant Stanley Girenas took off on a trans-Atlantic flight from Roosevelt Field, New York, in the Bellance monoplane *Lithuanica*. They were both experienced air-men and ex-service men. On July 17 the Associated Press wirelessed from Soldin, Pomerania, Germany, that their plane had crashed due to lack of fuel and that both fliers were dead. Startling rumors then began circulating and amazing discoveries were reported. It was said that the wrecked plane was found to contain fuel. It was said that the sheared tops of trees showed that it had come down under full power. Rumor had it that German troops seized parts of the debris of the plane and sealed them in a box-car and that these parts were never again seen. The bodies of the two fliers were hastily removed, according to this story, kept in soldered coffins; relatives were not permitted to see them for three months. When the bodies were at last viewed, it was thought that there were bullet-holes in the corpses which surgeons had tried to cover up. Newspapers in Poland, Belgium, Latvia and Russia boldly printed the declaration that these fliers were shot down by Nazi Storm Troopers in the belief that the ship was a Polish plane attempting to take photographs of a camp. The rumor still persists, and a startling light is thrown upon it by the fact that earlier two other planes, one from Poland and one from Latvia, mysteriously crashed within ten miles of the same spot.

would ask no other agent to undertake. The fastest boat is not fast enough. It's the only way."

CHAPTER 13
WINGS AGAINST TIME

BEACONS BLINKED on Boiling Field. In a line across one far corner, men stood on guard. Behind them sat a gigantic plane, its crew of five waiting alertly. Its four motors, capable of 3,000 horsepower, were warmed and idling. Its propellers, each tri-bladed, were spinning smoothly. In the winking light it sat, a magnificent, beautiful craft.

Floodlights glared as a motor droned overhead. Out of the night sky a small cabin plane swung. It eased down to a perfect landing. Immediately its tires touched, the floods blinked off again, and the giant S-42 was again shrouded in gloom. Out of the smaller plane, three passengers quickly alighted: a mild-mannered, middle-aged man, a bright-eyed girl, and a tough-looking boy with freckled face and pug-nose. An army officer marched toward them briskly.

"You must leave this field at once," he informed them. "Strict orders."

At that moment, a heavy sedan whirred from the gate of the airfield, cut straight across the spreading tarmac. Tim Donovan, turning away, saw light flash on two men in the front seat. He glimpsed features and his eyes opened wide. "That's Jimmy! Jimmy!"

The sedan sped on. When Tim hurried to follow the army

officer gripped his arm, dragged him to a stop. "You can't go over there!"

The Irish lad's answer was to snatch a glove from his left hand, raise before the officer's eyes the bright ring he wore, with its skull emblazoned against a black background, the mystic numeral 5 on the forehead. Operator 5 had designed that ring and presented it to the boy. Every United States Intelligence officer in the world had been informed that by it, Tim Donovan would be recognized as Operator 5's friend. The army officer peered at it in astonishment.

"I've been told about that! It's all right—go ahead! But these—"

Diane Elliot and John Christopher overruled the officer's objection by following Tim hurriedly. The boy broke into a run, shouting Operator 5's name. Jimmy Christopher turned from the cabin door of the giant plane to see him sprinting—to see Diane Elliot and ex-Operator Q-6 hastening after him. The boy came to a breathless, wide-eyed stop. "Jimmy! Dad and Di and I flew down from New York when we heard you were coming back to Washington! We just landed. Where're you going, Jimmy?"

"Glad to see you, Tim! Dad! Di!" He seized their hands warmly. "I couldn't wish for anything better than to see you again right now. I'm taking—"his face grew solemn, "a long hop. Not even the Commander of this ship will learn our destination until we have taken off."

"Jimmy!" Diane spoke quietly. "I know that light in your eyes. You know you're setting out to take some desperate chance.

Jimmy, I—I want to go with you. Wherever you're going, I want to go too."

"Di—it's impossible! You're game—you're grand to want to do it—but it's much too dangerous. Nor you either, Tim!" Operator 5 turned quickly as the boy began to plead. "This trip I'm going alone."

"Please, Jimmy!" the boy implored.

Operator 5's lips tightened. "No," he said quietly, "not this time, Tim... I've got to check up on equipment—it will take only a few minutes. Then I'll say goodbye."

HE STEPPED into the cabin of the huge plane. In the payload compartment, he found the apparatus he had requested to be put aboard. He checked each item quickly, gave crisp instructions to the crew, then stepped out again. He found his father standing alone near the steps.

"Dad—where's Tim and Di?"

"Perhaps, Jimmy, they found it too hard to say good-bye," John Christopher answered. "I would find it too hard myself. I'm not going to say it."

"You're not—?"

"I'm coming with you, Jimmy." The ex-operator's eyes gleamed with strong determination. "I can face any risk you face, son. As for something happening to me—" He smiled wanly. "These bullets near my heart—I know they may kill me at any moment. I'm an Intelligence man, Jimmy—it's in my blood. Rather than die in my chair, I want to die in the service. If this flight means my death—I'm willing to accept it."

Ex-Operator Q-6 quickly climbed the steps, entered the

cabin of the huge plane. Jimmy Christopher's eyes followed him with grave admiration. He snapped to alertness, uttered crisp orders to the crew. He turned to find Z-7 standing silently, eyeing him. He gripped the chief's hand.

"I'll keep in touch with you by radio, Chief. I'll wireless orders to our agents in Urakia during the flight. Finding the big gun and destroying it is only a hope, chief. But I'll do my best—"

Z-7's black eyes gazed with profound affection at Jimmy Christopher. His hand twined tightly in a warm, firm clasp. "Goodbye—and God be with you!"

Operator 5 stepped into the plane. The cabin door closed. Briskly he commanded: "Take off!"

Surging power beat from the four motors of the giant plane. Guards scattered out of its course. Its wings trembled as it began to move. Majestically it rolled across the smooth tarmac, gathering speed. Like a conqueror of the skies it drove with gargantuan power and magnificent ease, into the air. It shook thunder across the sky as it lifted into the hovering darkness of the night.

IN THE communications-room of WDC-13, the Washington chief sat tensely before the sensitive wireless receiver-transmitter which was tuned to the waveband of the S-42. He had returned immediately to the secret Intelligence Headquarters. He had caught the first reports flashing from the giant ship in flight. Pressing 'phones to his ears, he waited for further word from the radio operator aboard the great craft....

"Calling WDC-13! We are passing now over Ragged Harbor. We are flying through a terrific snow-storm, rising above it All is well. Ragged Harbor now left behind. We are rapidly passing out of sight of land. We are heading over the Atlantic at top speed."

"Over the Atlantic!" The most perilous stretch of the flight had begun. In the vastness of the sky, the lone plane was speeding. The world was unaware that over the Atlantic now wings were spreading, bent on a mission which held the fate of a great nation....

The drone of the motors, lost in the dark expanses of the night sky, sounded muffled within the cabin of the S-42. Peering through the ports, Jimmy Christopher saw only unlimited blackness. He had again checked all equipment, had again outlined orders to the crew. He paused near the radio equipment with John Christopher at his side.

The Commander of the S-42 stepped close, his eyes shining with dismayed astonishment.

"Sir, I am obliged to report that there are stowaways aboard!"

"What! Stowaways?"

"Two of them! I've just discovered them while inspecting the auxiliary fuel-tanks. They were hidden behind one of them. They—here they are, sir!"

Into the cabin—both smiling—stepped Tim Donovan and Diane Elliot! Operator 5 gazed at them in appalled surprise.

"Tim! Di! Good Lord! Whatever are—"

The girl hurried forward, eyes twinkling. "Jimmy Christopher, Tim and I decided that we wouldn't let you leave us behind! We made up our minds to come along—and we did! Just try to do something about it now!"

"Gee, Jimmy—don't be angry with us!" the Irish lad pleaded. "It was my idea."

Operator 5's throat tightened as he gazed at them. There was a determined, loyal, warm brightness in their eyes that clutched at his heart. Impulsively he reached to seize their hands.

"Are your orders to put back, sir, and to land and discharge these stowaways?" the Commander questioned.

"Your orders," Operator 5 answered, "are to proceed upon your course—at top speed!"

WINGS ACROSS the sea flying through deepest night. Unseen water below, unseen sky above—and the magic of radio following the course of the great plane across the world.

The wireless operator straightened, turned to Operator 5: "WDC-13, sir! Call for you!"

Operator 5 spoke briskly through the ether. Z-7's voice rang back through space: "It is just past midnight in the Eastern Standard time-zone! Another shell has just fallen in the very center of Philadelphia! There is terrific damage and loss of life! People are even more terrorized. The press is demanding an immediately extraordinary session of Congress—demanding that war be declared on Great Britain! Our only hope of avoiding it is the success of your mission!"

Swiftly eastward, flying against time! The long nerve-straining night passed slowly. Above the world, the sun soared, bringing brilliance to the expanse of the ocean, glinting upon the great wings which alone moved in all that limitless realm of sky and sea. Yet, appallingly soon, because the plane was speeding against the flight of the sun, the next report flashed through the ether from WDC-13.

"Calling Operator 5!" It was Z-7's rasped voice. "Another shell! It fell at noon, Central Standard Time, in St. Louis! The great bridge across the Mississippi is broken. Hysteria is now running rife through the country! The President is doing his utmost to reassure the people, but it is almost hopeless. Only one thing can reassure them—news that those damnable shells have ceased falling!"

Eastward! Beneath, on the sea, steamships. In the sky, great masses of white clouds becoming tinged with radiant color as the day waned. Roaring through space steadily, magnificently, the great plane followed its course into the growing dusk. Back across the vast ocean reports carried to WDC-13.

"S-42 reporting! We are approaching Ireland! If the plane continues without mishap, we will reach Urakia early in the morning."

Jimmy Christopher continued: "Z-7! We plan to reach Urol, the capital of Urakia, before the next shell is fired, even if it is timed to strike in the Eastern Standard Time belt of the United States. There will be an opportunity to make all our preparations and act before the zero hour. I am about to issue last-minute orders to our agents in Urakia!"

Operator 5 spoke then on the wavelength of the short-wave transmitter of a station within the borders of Urakia—a hidden installation used by the American Intelligence agents in that country to flash imperative reports to Washington. He called it anxiously. "UE! Calling UE! S-42 calling UE!"

Out of the growing night, a voice answered through the surging background static: "UE answering! Y-4 talking! We are awaiting orders!"

"Your investigation of the suspicious area is complete?"

"Yes! We have discovered a patrolled area in the woods south of Urol which was formerly unknown to us except as an ordinary military camp. It is a district in which cannon-reports have been heard, but thought to be ordinary artillery practice until your advice was received. We have further details which mean that the task of reaching the concealed gun will be extremely hazardous.

"ALL ROADS leading to the gun are patrolled. No one except certain officers of the Urakian Army are permitted to penetrate past guards at certain points. Within that area, we have observed a high wire fence which is charged with at least 20,000 volts of electricity. It completely encloses the gun location. We managed to reach that fence, but could not discover the gun. You have further orders?"

"Yes! You are to go at once to a place inside the patrolled section where this plane may land. Set out beacons which cannot be seen from the ground but which will be visible from the sky. Wait for the arrival of this ship there. We must make preparations immediately we land. We must lose no time in reaching the big gun before the next shell is fired."

"Yes, sir!"

"Bring with you, somehow, sufficient water to mix with a hundredweight of cement. Do this, if possible, by landing a plane beyond the sentry posts—a plane with a water-cooled engine which may be drained. All four agents are to hold themselves ready."

"Right!"

The S-42 flashed news that gladdened the hearts of the men in WDC-13:

"We are striking across Germany at a high elevation. So far as we are able to determine, we have not been observed."

In the cabin of the great S-42, as it soared through dark space, there was a hush disturbed only by the steady droning of the powerful motors. The auxiliary fuel supply had been valved into the main tanks. With silken smoothness, the engines were functioning. In the chart-room, Operator 5 made notations while Tim Donovan, Diane Elliot and John Christopher watched alertly.

Briskly, at last, he turned to the microphone. "Calling WDC-13! We are above Urakian territory! Urol lies straight ahead!"

Beneath the great plane, a few scattered lights gleamed. They marked villages and towns asleep in the rugged country of Urakia. In the very center of Europe the nation lay, massed about by the Great Powers, an imminent victim of their armed conflict. The Bulldog of Europe—slumbering!

Southward above the capital of Urakia the great plane swung. At Operator 5's order, its lights had been switched out. It was a great black bird coursing across a black sky and a black world. As the plane approached the point which Jimmy Christopher's calculations indicated to be the approximate location of the big gun, he peered downward into unbroken darkness—the vastness of a great wood.

The Commander waited at his side, alert for orders. In the darkness they stood as tense minutes passed. Tim Donovan listened for the first sound of Jimmy Christopher's voice. Diane Elliot watched the silhouette of his head against the port. The great plane banked slowly into a great, wide circle, its engines throttled down to a minimum....

Operator 5 straightened. "Lights below!"

In the sea of darkness beneath the S-42, twinkling beacons had appeared. Three of them, marking the points of a triangle—feeble gleams shooting high into the sky. Smartly Jimmy Christopher turned to the Commander. "Go down!

Over the microphone, Operator 5 spoke the words that the men in WDC-13, far across the Atlantic, had been waiting through nerve-wracking hours to hear: "We are about to land!"

CHAPTER 14
BIG-GUN VALEDICTORY

IN THE clearing in the woods south of Urol, thick darkness lay—darkness save for the three faint gleams shining skyward. They were invisible on the ground; they were shooting their light upward through metal tubes. In the sky above there was a whisking and a throaty rumble as a huge, black, winged form flitted across the sky—lowering....

From a shadow four men—United States Intelligence agents on duty in Urakia—watched....

Slowly the great bird circled and banked. It swung out of sight beyond the black foliage; when it reappeared, it swooped low. Motors off, lightless, it glided. Wind whistled as it descended; the tree-tops stirred. Then it winged into the blackness of the clearing.

Suddenly it became a motionless shadow in the night. It was down! For moments there was no suggestion of movement about it. It might have landed without a man aboard it, so still it sat. Nor did the four waiting men make the slightest motion until a footfall sounded.

Across the clearing strode a lone figure, blacker than the surrounding night. As it stopped, the four waiting men crept from their shelter. Slowly they approached, paused. A quiet question came at them: "Are you ready?"

"Ready!" One of the four stepped forward. "I am Y-4. This is Q-9. These are G-14 and V-20. Thank God you've landed safely!"

Jimmy Christopher's voice was quiet but tense. "Waste no time! The plane may have been heard! We must complete our preparations before any sentries can reach us. Unload immediately!"

The four men hurried toward the great plane. The crew worked quietly in the dark to assist them with the cargo. It was a strange load the S-42 had carried across the sea; and the orders issued by Operator 5, bewildering as they were, were carried out quickly and efficiently. "Inflate both balloons! Attach the collapsible baskets! Mix the cement in these canvas buckets and load them into one of the balloons! Attach this wire to the block of balsa—stick that knife into the wood firmly! Coil the hose and the funnel in the basket with the cement, this rope along with it! Nothing in this other basket except the other coil of rope!"

Into the quiet of the clearing sounded the hiss of compressed gas rushing from the metal tanks to inflate the balloons. Slowly the bags swelled as the baskets were staked down. They lolled in the wind, growing fatter and fatter, until Jimmy Christopher's command stopped the flow of helium.

"The wind is with us!" Y-4 exclaimed. "The enclosure is directly south of here—surrounded by the fence charged with high potential! Somewhere within that space the big gun is hidden!"

Operator 5 quickly made sure that all his instructions had been carried out. He called around him the four Intelligence agents and the crew of the S-42. Tim Donovan, John Christopher, and Diane Elliot stood close and listened anxiously.

"Both balloons are going up. We must manipulate the valves to keep them low, but high enough not to be seen by any guards. Once we are inside the enclosure, I will lower my bag to the ground. I will take off first, so that I will be able to bring your bag into position. Watch for a light signal. When you see it, lower the second balloon and drop the rope. Follow further orders as I give them. When you feel yourself cut free, open the tank valve and rise as quickly as possible."

TO THE crew of the S-42, Operator 5 commanded: "A take-off is barely possible from this clearing, and there is sufficient fuel to carry you to an airport across the Urakian borders. You will wait until daylight. If we do not return by that time, you are to resume flight. Upon landing, you are to state that this was an unannounced trans-Atlantic flight taken for commercial testing purposes. Here are your proper papers. The United States government must not be linked in any way with the S-42. Until dawn—wait! But no longer!"

He took Diane Elliot's firm, small hand in his. "Di—you must wait here with the plane. Your presence aboard it when it lands—if it lands without me—can be explained by your press connections. In no event, if this attempt is unsuccessful, is the Intelligence to be linked with the flight. Once the ship comes down again, you must return to the United States and forget that you ever knew Operator 5."

Jimmy Christopher turned away, his heart chilled as Diane's fingers drew from his. His commands sent two of the Intelligence agents into the basket loaded with mixed cement, with hosing and ropes. The second pair he ordered to the other. John Christopher strode alertly toward the first while Tim Donovan accompanied Operator 5 to the second. They climbed quickly into the carriages.

Diane Elliot stood back, alone in the darkness, watching the movements above the edge of the baskets. Her eyes were wide and welling with tears. She heard Operator 5's quiet commands, heard the rasp of a knife cutting through rope.

Silently, the balloon rose in the night air, swinging into the wind. Three men and a boy peered downward over the edge. One of them raised an arm in a farewell signal—Jimmy Christopher.

Unseen in the darkness, Diane Elliot pressed her red lips tightly together and watched the balloon soar into the darkness....

With the valve-rope in his hand, Jimmy Christopher studied the spread below. No man in the basket spoke while the balloon wafted slowly southward in the wind. Tim Donovan stood close at Operator 5's side as black tree-tops bleared past. Long minutes passed before Y-4 spoke quietly.

"We're drifting over an artificial clearing! There—below—the charged fence!"

It was dimly visible—a black line in the deeper blackness of the ground. From below sounded the faint rhythm of footfalls. Along the fence, almost invisible, a sentry was marching, rifle across his shoulder. He paced on evenly as the balloon drifted slowly into the space enclosed by the high-potential barrier.

"To touch that fence would mean sure death!" Y-4 whispered. "There must be more sentries posted somewhere inside to watch the movements of the gun-crew. Somewhere below, that cannon is hidden!"

Operator 5 looked down upon a spread of ground that had been stripped of trees. Ragged stumps dotted the earth. In all directions the artificial clearing spread, bordering the charged wire. A faint luminescence sometimes played along the high potential web, marking the boundary. Jimmy Christopher stood alert, peering down, until he judged that the balloon was floating slowly over the center of the huge square.

"Now!"

HE RELEASED the valve of the rippling bag. Gas hissed out. The basket began to swing lower. As it descended, Jimmy

Christopher raised a coil of rope, making sure that its one end was firmly anchored. Quickly, then, he tossed the rope overside. He swung over the rim of the basket, gripping it, lowering himself. "Listen for orders!"

He peered downward to see the balloon wafting low across the ground, the end of the rope trailing. Hand over hand he went down as the wind soughed past him, until he was dangling close above the ground. His hands loosened; he dropped.

Instantly be whirled, looping the slack of the rope, whipping the noose about a stump. The strand snapped tight and whined. Operator 5 paused, peering about alertly, hand sliding toward his automatic He stood motionless until a rustle sounded above him. He jerked eyes upward to see a small figure sliding down the tightrope.

"I had to come with you, Jimmy!"

Operator 5 answered grimly. "You're down now, Tim! Stout fella! Stick close! If you spot any sentry coming—climb that rope as fast as you can. Eyes sharp!"

Jimmy Christopher peered up past the anchored balloon. Against the blackness of the sky a small cloud was drifting— the second bag. He followed its course across the clearing after it passed the high-potential wire. When it was drifting directly overhead, he brought his torch into his hand, touched the button.

Signal!

A hissing sounded overhead—gas flowing through the opened valve of the second balloon. It drifted lower. The dark figures visible over the edge of the basket moved quickly. Down from the air a rope coiled, snaking to the ground. Operator 5 sprang after it. Tim Donovan's tough hands seized it the same instant. Swiftly they looped the slack, snagged the rope around a stump. The balloon hung almost motionless above them.

"Now, Tim! With me!"

"Jimmy!" The boy's whisper was quick, breathless. "Jimmy, look!"

His stubby finger pointed toward a faint glow on the ground ahead. It was scarcely visible; it seemed to be shining through the surface of the ground. Operator 5 moved silently toward it He paused, noting heaped branches ahead—branches torn from felled trees and scattered over the ground. With the utmost care he lifted those that lay in his path to the light, and shifted them aside, to clear the way.

Each move he made was quick, yet sure; always he was alert for any sound that might betray the approach of a sentry. Little by little, as Tim Donovan helped, he opened the path toward the light He saw now that it was gleaming through a thicker heap of branches. When he paused, the shine reflecting in his eyes, he saw a huge, metallic tube protruding through them at an angle—thick-watted, glistening, a sinister black.

Motionless, Operator 5 peered into it—the maw of the Urakian gun!

FAR-AWAY VOICES, echoing with a hollow ring, sounded in the silence. Jimmy Christopher moved alertly, quickly, cautiously. With the utmost care he lifted aside a branch while its dried leaves rustled quietly; he stepped into the space he had cleared. Again he looked into the shining barrel of the huge cannon, into black depths from which deadly explosive had been flung high into the stratosphere, across an ocean, to plunge to earth amid a terror-stricken people.

The distant voices drew him toward the great circular opening through which the muzzle of the cannon protruded. He lowered himself flat, eased forward to peer in a vast hollow hewn in rock—looked along the amazingly long, black barrel. He gazed upon the most tremendous weapon ever devised by the mind and hand of man.

Its size dwarfed the uniformed crew who were moving about its base. The sleek, wire-wound tube was supported by a tremendous carriage gleaming in brilliant light. Bolts thick as a man's body pinioned it to its holdfast of solid rock; studs as large as tables, waist-high, were turned hard against the gigantic flanges. Glistening rods of the recoil mechanism were of huge proportions; beside it great compressed-air recuperators poised like tilted tanks. Near the walls, immense electric motors were belted to machinery which shifted the barrel of the gun for elevation and traversing. Above the massive breech, movable on overhead tracks, electric derricks poised for charge—and shell-hoisting. A score of dials marked by slender indicators registered the delicate adjustments of the incredible weapon. It sat deep beneath the surface of the earth while only its snout protruded into the open.

A grim admiration filled Operator 5 as he observed the terrible magnificence of the Urakian gun. The chamber in which it was housed was a vast space hewn out of solid rock, its walls concrete and smooth as paper. He saw that the roof of the chamber was of sheet iron rigidly reinforced, on movable rollers so that it could be shifted as the elevation of the barrel was altered. He noted, below, steel doors set into the walls which, when they opened to pass uniformed members of the gun-crew, disclosed still other safety-doors beyond. And in the great hollow, commands rang as the crew worked.

Men were making adjustments at the valves of the tremendous hydraulic buffer in accordance with the orders of an under-officer. Others were swarming toward the breech of the massive piece. A clattering sound came as steel doors opened, and a motorized cradle rolled into the room, carrying shining silk bags—bags of propellant. Another door opened to admit another cradle which carried a shell into sight! Under Operator 5's eyes lay a gigantic projectile intended to pierce the highest sky and plunge to an unknown mark somewhere in America!

He glanced at his watch quickly. The exact instant of the discharge of the big gun, he knew, depended upon the location of its chosen target; but this was a matter of time measurable in seconds. It was nearing five a.m.—the approximate time the gun must be fired if its shell were to fall anywhere within the Eastern Standard time-zone of the United States. The fact that the loading crew of the gun were in action now meant that the next target was certainly somewhere within that region. A matter of minutes and again doom would go streaking across the sky, the comet of destruction would plunge out of the night upon hysterical Americans!...

THE MOTORIZED shell truck approached the great breech of the gun. The tapered nose of the gigantic projectile glistened brightly. At an officer's command, the percussion cap

Downward through the hose the soft cement oozed into

the mouth of the huge underground cannon.

was screwed into place. An overhead crane whirred; chains clanked downward. Next the shell rose in the air, swinging gently, while commands barked and the crew strove to swing it to the breech of the cannon.

Operator 5 drew back grimly. He was about to rise when new voices ringing from below reached his ears. Again he looked down, to see a steel door opening. A huge officer in resplendent uniform was entering with a woman. He was obviously the commander of the gun. The woman moved gracefully, one slender hand holding the fur collar of her coat about her face. In the vast chamber she was a tiny figure—but a figure that Operator 5 recognized instantly—Radi Havara!

Her presence at the gun amazed Operator 5; but he recalled information sent to M-11 about the woman spy which offered a clear explanation. The mysterious plane guarded in its hangar at Roosevelt field—and the woman seen getting into it! That she had undertaken, as a means of escape, a dangerous transoceanic flight was certain. It was a daring act fully in keeping with her character. Her landing in Urakia, Jimmy Christopher realized, had preceded his by almost a full day. She stood below him now, at the aide of the commander of the gun, and her glinting eyes turned upon its magnificence.

Through the rattling of the machinery, across the hollow of the chamber, the voice of the Commander echoed: "It is only proper that you should be accorded the privilege of viewing this beautiful weapon—a privilege denied all but my staff and the members of the crew. Some of the more conservative high officials of Urakia do not even know that this gun exists. We built it and installed it secretly. No doubt those officials would be amazed and dismayed to learn of the use to which it is being put. Yet, behold it! The mightiest cannon ever built by humans—a weapon to save Urakia from destruction! It is you who have made the achievement of our cause possible!"

The woman's soft answer was lost in the clatter; Operator 5 half rose, still peering at her.

"You may justly admire every detail," the Commander continued, "for each has been planned with meticulous care. The underground passages by which the crew comes and goes. The underground barracks, modern in every respect. Our power-plant, wireless station and provisions for communication—the powder magazines, protected by many safety doors, and the shell stores. Yet these, magnificent as they are, do not testify to the skill with which the gun is operated.

"Every factor is taken into consideration. The barometric pressure at all points along the trajectory of the shell is computed and allowance is made. The elevation of the point of burst above sea level is taken into consideration. The charts we use for aiming are the most accurate in the world. Each separate charge of superite is chemically analyzed here, just before the propellant is rammed into the gun, and the results allowed for. Our electric control beam is stabilized by the most accurate Piezo crystal in existence. We have taken every precaution to assure perfect accuracy in our fire. We have achieved a perfection hitherto thought impossible. Perfection, ah! You shall see!"

THE GREAT shell had been thrust into the gigantic bore by an electrically-operated ram. The charge cradle was swinging into position so that the silken bags of superite could be driven home next. Preparations for the firing of the gun were going on smoothly and swiftly.

Operator 5 rose quickly. He drifted to a position beneath the second balloon while Tim Donovan kept at his side. He called softly to the men in the dangling basket: "Lower the balsa block!"

Over the side of the basket, the huge block appeared. It dropped downward, swinging at the end of a wire. Jimmy Christopher seized it, and as the wire was played out from the basket, carried it toward the muzzle of the gun. He pulled the knife from the soft wood, quickly estimated the diameter of the gun-bore, and began to carve. The pulpy fragments fell away as he cut the block to a circle.

The commander's voice was audible below; he was still speaking to Radi Havara: "Very soon, now! In a few minutes we will fire! All computations have been made; the elevation and traverse position are set! At the proper second, the great shell will fly on its way. Its target this time—you know? It is the Capitol of the United States! Directly upon the great dome that shell will fall!"

Jimmy Christopher's heart chilled as he heard the words. Desperately he worked to cut the block into a thick wafer. From below, the voice of the commander still carried.

"You will see the great gun fire! You will hear the shell sing high into the sky—into the most rarefied air at terrific speed—to vanish. Then—at exactly the second of midnight, it will plunge to its mark. The Capitol will crumble into wreckage! And the

United States still believes that Great Britain is its aggressor! There can be but one result of tonight's shell—immediate war!"

Jimmy Christopher rose from the breathless work of trimming the Balsa block. Making sure that the wire was firmly affixed to the eye-bolt which was fastened tight at its center, he carried it to the muzzle of the gun. He reached high to fit it; he lowered it; he trimmed the wood again. After moments of terrific work he again lifted the block to the bore.

With all his weight he pressed against it. The soft wood yielded to the steel of the gun. The rifling bit through the fibers; it fitted tightly. Operator 5 shoved it into the muzzle as far as he could reach—anchored the wire to hold it. He backed away as the voice of the commander carried up:

"Within five minutes the electric timer will pull the firing lanyard! At the exact fraction of a second! All is ready now. Nothing is to be awaited for! The instant comes—a jerk on the lanyard—and it is done!"

Within five minutes!... Operator 5 turned from the gun. Tim Donovan hastened breathlessly with him again as he ran to the rope, pinioning the second balloon to the earth. He un-looped it from the stump, ordered: "Release gas!" The black bag riffled as the valve hissed open. Gripping the rope, with Tim Donovan aiding him, he struggled across the ground. The buoyancy of the balloon threatened to lift them, but the continuously released gas enabled them to drift the bag closer to the muzzle of the cannon. Again he snagged the rope.

"Drop the hose!" Operator 5 hissed. "Start the cement flowing when I give a light-signal!"

CHAPTER 15
THE FATE OF A NATION

FROM THE dangling basket, a thick black tube snaked down. John Christopher released it, leaning over the edge to watch Operator 5's operations. Jimmy Christopher seized it, turned its lower end into the muzzle of the cannon until it rested against the balsa block. Glancing about alertly, he commanded Tim to raise the hose off the ground. Then he signaled with his torch.

Downward through the hose, as the collapsible buckets in the basket were emptied into a huge funnel, the soft cement poured. Viscidly, it streamed from the open lower end of the tube, collecting against the balsa block, its level mounting. The flow was slow; precious minutes ticked past while Operator 5 spread the mixture. From below, the commander's voice still rumbled: "Two minutes now—a little less! You are quite safe here, Miss Havara. You will be astonished that the report is no louder than it is. We have applied new principles so that most of the sound vibrations of the explosion are transformed into supersonic impulses—wave-lengths inaudible to the human ear. Yet the explosion comes with gigantic power. Again and again, when it flies through its trajectory accurately controlled by our radio-beam, explosions occur within the shell to drive it on its way. One slight movement of the lanyard and all that tremendous power is set loose. It is not long now!"

Jimmy Christopher withdrew the end of the hose as the level of the heavy cement mounted in the gun-bore. He flung it aside when the stuff dripped out of the lip of the muzzle. He stepped back, knife in hand, and seized the rope holding the balloon to the earth.

The blade cut through the strand. The rope trailed off as the balloon began to drift. Above sounded a sharp, steady hiss. From a condensed-gas tank, helium was flowing into the envelope, swelling it, swiftening its rise. It wafted up against the black sky, a diminishing cloud, melting into the gloom of the night.

"With me, Tim?" Operator 5 started along the lane he had cleared through the branches. The Irish lad's hand sought his arm. In the quiet, as they walked, Tim asked: "Gee, Jimmy—what've you done?"

"Simply plugged the barrel, Tim. You would imagine that the plug of balsa wood would vanish in splinters the instant the charge exploded. You would think that even the heavy cement would offer no obstacle to the passage of the shell from the barrel. But the plug will more than stop the shell, Tim. The inertia of that weight in the muzzle will act the same as wet earth packed into the bore of a high-power rifle, as has happened when hunters have carelessly stood their gun muzzle down on soft dirt. The terrific force of the explosion, meeting that obstacle, will turn back and—"

"Jimmy!" The boy gasped the quick warning and twisted to stare at lights the gloom. The frantic boy dropped low when lights flashing within the enclosure of the high-potential wire. The beams swung brilliantly in the hands of running men. Voices called hoarsely. From two sides, lights appeared—swinging up. In the shafts glistened the bag of the second pinioned balloon.

"There!" a voice called. "I told you I saw! Someone is in here!"

"Waste no time!" another called. "Shoot it down first! Find them when it drops! Quick!"

OPERATOR 5'S hand flashed to the armpit holster of his automatic. Dark forms—guards—were running toward the spot at which the balloon was anchored. Their rifles glinted in the reflected light of their electric torches. Jimmy Christopher saw one of them stop, raise a rifle to fire full into the silken bag rolling overhead.

Operator 5's gun flashed level. The destruction of the balloon, he realized only too well, would eliminate their only possible escape. He aimed instantly. His fingers tightened three times, swiftly, on the trigger.

The sharp reports echoed into a scream—into hoarse cries of consternation. One light-beam shafted upon the rifleman who had raised his weapon to fire into the balloon. He was spinning, dropping. The bullet from Operator 5's automatic had sped true. He screamed again as he fell. Other guards leaped with their lights swinging in a swift search.

Operator 5 sprang aside, tugging the Irish lad after him. "Tim! Get to that rope if you can! Get into that basket and cast off! If you're not out of this space by the time the timer pulls the lanyard, you'll be killed instantly!"

Operator 5 thrust at the boy, forcing him into a desperate run. Instantly he whirled, and as Tim Donovan stopped, staring back in agony, he melted away in the gloom. The frantic boy dropped low when the light-beams swung toward him; he leaped up as the shafts moved on. Recklessly he ran, agile as a young deer, leaping across stumps, ducking low again, circling wildly toward the spot where the balloon was held by the rope.

Commands roared from the dark. "Find them now! Kill them! They will not be able to use that balloon if you shoot straight!"

The guards were spreading out; others were running to join them. The darkness, cut by the swinging shafts, became a hideous confusion in which Tim Donovan could see no sign of Operator 5. He dodged from stump to stump, breathlessly, searching for Jimmy Christopher, hearing again in his mind the imperative warning: "If you're not out of this space by the time the timer pulls the lanyard, you'll be killed instantly!"

Tim Donovan's only thought, as he scampered in spurts toward the spot beneath the balloon, was not that he would be killed; he could think only that Jimmy Christopher was nowhere near the balloon—was still within the boundaries of death.

The Irish lad darted swiftly toward the stump to which the taut rope was tied. He sprang into the shadow of the balloon while the guards scattered beyond. He gripped the rope, peered around frantically. As he sensed a movement in the darkness, his heart leaped.

"Jimmy!"

A snarl answered as a dark figure leaped toward the boy. A gun-barrel glinted its threat. A uniformed Urakian officer sprang forward to strike a vicious blow. It cut Tim Donovan cruelly across the face, staggered him backward. He stumbled to a stop, sobbing, as the officer started to strike again. With the fury of a young wild-cat be leaped.

HE STRUCK with all his strength at the hand gripping

the huge automatic. He bounded upon the officer with both fists swinging. His knuckles cracked raw into the uniformed man's face as a savage arm-swing struck him away. He dropped again—saw the gun swinging toward him. Above it shone a white face twisted with fury. Tim Donovan cringed back, eyes closed, stunned—waiting for the bullet to come....

A strangled gasp startled him. He sprang up to see the officer being dragged backward. An arm was circling the man's neck. He was twisted aside, and Tim Donovan saw Jimmy Christopher pinioning him from the rear. A choking sob tore from the boy's lips when he saw the officer tear away, saw the gun flash.

Operator 5's blow was lightning swift. It drove to the point of the officer's chin. He followed as the uniformed man toppled; he struck a second blow to the neck. The Urakian fell—paralyzed by a jiu-jitsu thrust. Operator 5 spun away.

"Tim! They're coming back! Climb that rope!"

The boy seized the rope in cold hands, pulled himself up as he glimpsed lights flashing closer, dark figures running straight toward the spot. The sounds of the struggle had turned the guards back on their tracks. Their weapons glinted in the shafting beams as Tim lifted himself.

"Jimmy! Jimmy—*quick!*"

Operator 5's automatic blazed swift fire. He sent slugs blazing at the swarming guards until he emptied his clip. Two of the men stumbled and fell with punctured legs; another sprawled face down, howling with the agony of a broken shoulder. Three others stopped, leveling their rifles; the others rushed on.

Operator 5 whirled to the rope. He gripped it, pulled himself up swiftly. In his left hand he was still clasping the knife that had released the first balloon. He swung it now to the strand below him. One quick slice severed it. The balloon bobbed free, rising, swinging into the wind, while Operator 5 clung there.

Spiteful rifle-fire broke out below as he dropped the knife and pulled himself up. Wind soughed past him as the balloon lifted. Above him, Tim Donovan was climbing desperately.

With all the strength he possessed, the boy jerked himself higher. Breath beat in and out of his burning lungs. His hands were rawed by the rough strand. Bit by bit he struggled higher, until the lower edge of the basket was level with his head, until he could reach and grip the rim. He dragged himself over, dropped into the basket. Desperately he grasped the valve of the compressed-gas tank and turned it full on.

Helium hissed into the bag; its speed of ascent quickened. Peering overside, Tim Donovan saw Operator 5 climbing the swinging rope. Below its whipping end, on the open spread of ground, lights were still flashing upward, flicking across Jimmy Christopher. Rifles snapped again in a spiteful attack. Even faster the balloon whisped upward as Operator 5 reached to grip the edge of the basket and swing in.

THROUGH TWO slashes in Operator 5's coat, red was flowing. He drew a deep breath as he peered down at the black ground, tightened his arm across the Irish lad's shoulder.

"They hit me, Tim—but I'm okay! Valve full on? We're rising as fast as we can. Steady, old-timer! Hold onto yourself! In a second—"

Suddenly, terrifically, the earth was shaken by a tearing concussion.

The force of the blast ripped through the sky to envelope the balloon carrying Operator 5 and Tim Donovan. Cyclonic winds tossed it, swung its basket erratically. Clouds of vapor gusted up to smother it. Through a mighty confusion, in the midst of holocaustic turmoil, it was lashed and buffeted and snatched by the forces of destructive power. Beneath the edge of the basket, Operator 5 and Tim Donovan crouched as the fury tore around them....

They rose dizzily in the swinging carriage to peer down through hazy air. The explosion had ignited the foliage of the surrounding trees. Flickering flames were bordering the area that had been enclosed by the web of high-potential wires. The fence was broken. The ground was heaped with raw earth. In the midst of that black scene, the space that had been the gun-pit was visible.

Its cement walls had crumbled down to fill it with ragged boulders. From them, the snout of the huge weapon protruded. The length of its barrel was opened by a great long gash through which the imprisoned superite had burst. Balked by the plug in the muzzle, the terrific force of the propellant had torn through the steel and out the breech. By its own power the gun had been destroyed....

Operator 5 spoke quietly.

"The Urakian gun has fired its last shell, old-timer. Radi Havara has met her end with it...."

THE S.S. *ULTIMA*, steaming under an azure sky, moved

majestically across New York Bay. Her rails were crowded with hundreds of passengers watching the spires of the Manhattan skyscrapers glisten in the sun. She had made a swift run from Liverpool; her journey was almost at an end.

In the salon, Operator 5 stood reading the latest wireless dispatches that had been posted. Tim Donovan was at one side, Diane Elliot at the other. John Christopher leaned to read across his shoulder:

> Washington—International negotiations have proceeded rapidly since the cessation of the artillery attacks upon the United States. For the first time in history, the secret archives of the government have been opened in order to inform the people of the true state of affairs. The revelations are startling.
>
> Following the announcement by the President that the big gun has been destroyed, that the United States is no longer in danger of renewed attacks, the Chief Executive announced today that the responsibility lies not with Great Britain, as was at first believed, but with Urakia.
>
> Already negotiations have been completed whereby Urakia will pay to the United States government a vast sum in reparations. The nation, declared the President, win not answer the attacks with a declaration of war, since that would only add to the tragedy of the occurrence.

Tim Donovan turned away to read again a radiogram that had been delivered to Operator 5 during the voyage. His eyes shone brightly.

Please do me the honor of visiting me as soon as possible after your arrival so that I may express, ineffectively as I must, the undying gratitude that is in my heart for your unequalled services to your country.

The name affixed was that of the President of the United States.

Diane Elliot tugged happily at Jimmy Christopher's arm. They strode upon deck, into the bright sunlight, as the great ship edged closer to Manhattan. With Diane and Tim beside him, Operator 5 gazed through the clear sunlight at Liberty raising her torch, bidding her welcome to a nation freed of danger, blessed with peace....